LADY VIOLET ENJOYS A FROLIC

THE LADY VIOLET MYSTERIES—BOOK FOUR

GRACE BURROWES

GRACE BURROWES PUBLISHING

DEDICATION

**This series is dedicated
to my nephew, Jackson**

CHAPTER ONE

The greatest mistake of my life had been submitting to the authority of a husband simply to escape the authority of my father.

As a widow of means, I wanted to be very certain of my motivations before I embarked on a second marital journey.

My travels northward to Scotland with Hugh St. Sevier had been trying in the extreme, largely because he and I had not yet become lovers. Our journey south was going by much too rapidly to suit me, in part because we were now intimates. I had no wish to return to London, where my conscientiously attentive vicar, curious domestic staff, and compulsively nosy neighbors would all remark my closer friendship with St. Sevier.

I had given Hugh permission to pay me his addresses, but as my traveling coach rolled through Cumberland and then Westmoreland counties, I had time—far too much time—to question my decision. My first marriage had been trying for all concerned. I wasn't ready to leap into a second, even with Hugh, whom I adored more ardently the longer I knew him.

To my great delight, our return to London was to be delayed by a detour into the Lake District.

"Tell me about our host," I said, pulling off my gloves and unlacing my boots as the traveling coach swayed out of the innyard. "Was he your commanding officer?"

"Lord Rutland was not exactly my commanding officer," St. Sevier said. "He was Colonel Damien Rutherford then, and I was a medical volunteer. I was technically answerable to a separate chain of command, but I served under Rutherford nonetheless. He is married to the former Athena Grossnickel, heiress to the Grossnickel wealth and daughter of General Octavian Grossnickel."

I was a veteran of half a dozen London Seasons and an earl's daughter. I had heard of the Grossnickels, a fine old Derbyshire family with a sizable coal fortune.

"She would be several years older than I am," I said, "but I don't believe she made a proper come out."

"Mrs. Grossnickel followed the drum, and the children with her. Athena has two sisters, and no brothers."

Hence the heiress designation. "Were you sweet on the fair Athena?"

St. Sevier's smile was wistful, turning a handsome countenance gorgeous. "We were all in love with Athena, but given that I am French, my loyalties were always suspect among the English. I worshipped from afar, until I met my Annie. Dare I hope you are preparing to nap so early in the day, Violet?"

"Your hopes are your business," I said, untying my bonnet ribbons and setting my hat on the opposite bench. "I intend to be comfortable. Who else from your old regiment lives in the area?"

"Thomas MacNeil, our quartermaster, serves as Lord Rutland's senior steward. MacNeil was part magician, part abacus. Whether we needed horse blankets or cooking pots, he had an amazing ability to conjure goods from thin air. He wasn't as successful with medical supplies, but then, nobody was. MacNeil is a quiet sort, salt of the earth. An easy man to like."

Hugh was easy to like, easy on the eye, and also an easy man to love. He was slightly more than six feet of French good looks, with wavy chestnut hair, dark brown eyes, and a smile that made me believe in every good, sweet thing fate had yet to reveal. Hugh was also slow to judge his fellow mortal and slower to anger. When he was truly in a temper, his rage was cold, which I much preferred to silly drama staged to garner undeserved attention.

Life had not always been kind to him—he had lost a spouse in Spain—and yet, he had a bone-deep decency that contrasted with the exquisite manners and flexible morals my late husband had exhibited. Freddie had been charming, but Freddie's charm had been deployed as a weapon, to manipulate. Hugh charmed for the pleasure of being agreeable company.

In the manner of many aristocratic French sons, Hugh had been sent for safekeeping to relatives in England as the French revolution had been followed by successive governments, the Reign of Terror, intrigues at the highest level, wars, and finally, the rise of Napoleon Bonaparte.

Several of Hugh's siblings had died fighting for *l'empereur,* while Hugh had trained as a physician in Scotland. His medical knowledge was extensive, and he'd served with Wellington's army willingly, patching up French and English soldiers alike, as did his French counterparts.

"Did Lord Rutland and MacNeil know your late wife?" I asked.

"They did, not well. Annie got on poorly with the other women, and our union was as stormy as it was brief. Shall I fold out the benches, my lady?"

I curled down against him, pillowing my head on his muscular thigh. "If you fold out the benches, I will be tempted to take liberties with your person. Lady Rutland will probably house me two floors and a guest wing apart from you. I am not looking forward to observing the proprieties, St. Sevier."

He stroked my hair gently. "Scotland was lovely."

In Scotland, we had been the guests of an old school friend of mine, and she had billeted us in the former laird and lady's private apartment—the best guest rooms she could offer. We'd had separate bedrooms—should we desire to use them—and only a private sitting room between them.

"Scotland was scrumptious," I said, resisting the urge to move into Hugh's touch. St. Sevier was affectionate by nature, one of many reasons I cherished him. "I really do not want to return to London, Hugh."

"Are you afraid I will abandon you in Town?"

I was both afraid I would lose my nerve for frolicking when back in my familiar surroundings and afraid that fate would snatch Hugh from me, as Freddie had been snatched from me. I hadn't been in love with Freddie, but neither had I expected him to expire after a mere five years of marriage.

"I have enjoyed the privacy we've shared during our travels," I said. "Have you ever been to the Lakes before?"

He grasped my hand and kissed my knuckles. "I will not abandon you when we return to London, *mon coeur*. I will court you with equal parts passion and gentlemanly discretion. I have not been to the Lakes previously, to answer your question, and I look forward to seeing the area with you. Long walks, picnics, excursions on horseback, and lazy afternoons with a fishing pole are on the itinerary I have planned for us."

"And naps?"

"Napping is part of picnicking, I'm told. Do you truly dread returning to London so much, Violet?"

I did, though I wasn't sure why. Spring was London's best season, according to many, and I would hardly have time to unpack my trunks in Town before I was due to nip out to Surrey to attend the christening of the first Deerfield grandson. I was to be godmother to my brother Felix's firstborn, a bittersweet honor when I'd been unable to present Freddie with any children.

"I was unhappy in Town," I said, "as a bride, a wife, and a widow."

"Then don't bide in Town, Violet. Life is short and uncertain. Bide where you are happy. Are you sure you don't want to fold out the benches? I asked John Coachman to make a leisurely progress for this leg of our journey. Even taking our time, we will likely reach Rutland Wood by midafternoon."

At the pace we were going, a change of teams would not be needed for at least another hour and a half.

"I am not in an amorous mood," I said, "meaning no reflection on present company."

"You are pensive," St. Sevier said, pulling off his boots. "We will have a cuddle and a nap and arrive refreshed to our destination."

We had the business of folding out the benches to make a bed of the coach's interior down to a science, and once I was sprawled against St. Sevier's side, I found my eyes growing heavy. Hugh, true to his word, held me while I slept, and yet, when he handed me down at Rutland Wood later that day, I still felt far from refreshed.

Had anybody told me that my host, Damien, Lord Rutland, had charm to eclipse even the vast stores St. Sevier claimed, I would not have believed them. His lordship was no boy, his blue eyes having crow's feet, his countenance being a trifle weathered. His physique was trim and muscular, though he lacked a few inches of St. Sevier's height, and the barest thread of silver graced his temples.

His smile was nonetheless the warmest, friendliest, merriest specimen I had encountered in many a year. Faint echoes of my late husband's insouciance echoed in that smile, as did the ability to create an instant conspiracy of two against all the world's seriousness and woe.

"Lady Violet will want a tour of the gardens, I hope," his lordship said, tucking my hand over his arm and escorting me up the two dozen terraced steps leading to a wide front portico. "You may rest your weary bones, St. Sevier, for I intend to take her ladyship captive."

St. Sevier merely cocked his head, silently asking me if I was willing to *be* captured.

How well he knew me, already. "St. Sevier will find his way to your library, my lord, and plunder all of your botanical pamphlets and medical treatises. I will accompany you on a tour of the garden, the better to abet your truancy from correspondence, ledgers, and other duties." Also to *move* after hours of drowsing in the coach.

"You have found me out," his lordship said, patting my knuckles. "I do adore a discerning woman."

He ushered us into the house, though *house* was too modest a term for the vast edifice his lordship called home. Our steps echoed in a soaring circular foyer, and afternoon light poured in through tall windows and a central skylight. White marble floors, alabaster statuary, and portraits in gilt frames all added to a sense of grandeur, though having grown up in a rambling country house myself, all I could think was that in winter, the foyer would be an icehouse.

And white floors showed every speck of dirt.

We commended St. Sevier into the keeping of a pretty, mobcapped housekeeper whose smile was genuinely cheerful. Perhaps the crisp northern air made the locals happy, just as London's smoke made the capital's denizens ill.

St. Sevier sent me a wink over his shoulder, and I was abandoned into Lord Rutland's keeping. I should not have minded that I had no idea where Hugh would sleep or how to find him, but two years of mourning had left me with nervous tendencies. I thus admitted to a slight anxiety as I saw him disappear up a majestic curving staircase.

"Away with us," Lord Rutland said, taking my hand and replacing it on his arm. "A soldier learns to treasure the fine weather, because the other kind inevitably comes around at the most inconvenient moment. The gardens are just beginning to bloom, and Athena and I are insufferably proud of them."

"Do you miss army life?" I asked as he led me into a corridor that opened off the foyer. An abundance of windows—one might even say an extravagance of windows—filled even this part of the house with sunlight and warmth. The corridor begged for green plants and for the occasional napping cat, but instead held more art.

"I miss army life probably in the same way you miss the Season you made your come out. You have memories of that time gilded with a fond, inaccurate patina. You made great friendships that you will treasure into old age, and yet, you would not wish that same ordeal on anybody you cared for."

He'd got the last part right.

"Tell me, Lady Violet, how does my friend St. Sevier honestly fare?"

The question took me somewhat aback, for I was not Hugh's wife, nor even his official intended, that my counsel on the subject of his wellbeing should have been sought.

"He is well," I said, which was true. Hugh enjoyed roaring good physical health and impressive animal spirits. "As far as I know, Monsieur is happily settled into civilian life."

"His situation was difficult." Lord Rutland ushered me through another door onto a sprawling back terrace. "He served well, despite all, and his facility with the French and Spanish languages was abundantly useful. Welcome to my garden, Lady Violet."

I stepped out into the sunlight and was immediately aware of the scent of the forest rising up behind the house.

Forests in southern England tended to roll placidly along next to farmland, tamed in antiquity and put in service to civilization. Many had been reduced to mere home wood status, providing fuel, game, and timber for a specific estate.

In contrast to that sylvan domesticity, Rutland Wood manor was enthroned before high hills blanketed with tall conifers. The forest remained primeval here, dense, dark, and imposing, despite the grand gleaming manor seated on its border. Oaks and other hardwoods lined paths to the stables and outbuildings, but I had no doubt that given a few generations of freedom, the mountain forest would swallow every evidence of man's encroachment.

Perhaps Rutland enjoyed the challenge of keeping nature

battled into submission, for the struggle would be endless. Formal parterres were lined with brilliant beds of tulips in a repeating pattern of red, yellow, and white. A few precocious irises—alternating beds of purple and yellow—lined up along the central walkway, and faded daffodils had been subdued into tidy bundles along the peripheries.

"How delightful," I said, resisting the urge to shake free of my escort and wander at will. His lordship would march me up and down the rows, I was certain. We'd move sedately and smiling all the while, but we'd travel the route of his choosing at the pace he set.

"Athena loves her garden," Lord Rutland said, "and I love Athena, hence we indulge our gardeners."

A profession of husbandly devotion ought to have charmed me. I instead found it a trifle gauche. A man should *show* the world he loved his lady rather than bandy the words so genially before a near stranger. Freddie had been full of adoring words as he'd slipped out the door to cavort with his mistresses.

Or perhaps a devoted husband ought to do both—make the professions and perform the devoted deeds. I was hardly a qualified judge of marital romance.

"Your garden reminds me of one facet of London life that pales compared to rural splendors," I said. "And how I adore the scent of the pines. I'm put in mind of my recent stay in Perthshire."

Though in central Scotland, the forest had a more stately quality, perhaps because the conifers were enormous and thus spaced more widely.

"Did you enjoy your time up north?" Lord Rutland asked, leading me down the steps.

"Very much. The people are quite friendly, the scenery breathtaking. I did not want to leave."

St. Sevier had escorted me north to attend a friend's wedding, and he and I had got more than we bargained for in terms of prenuptial intrigue. I had also seen, for the first time, the ancestral home of Sebastian MacHeath, Marquess of Dunkeld. Sebastian had been a

dear acquaintance of my youth, but military service and misunderstandings had parted us.

I had only recently begun to rebuild my friendship with the
marquess, and I hoped in future to continue with the project.

"I did not want to leave Rutland Wood," my host said, starting me
down a path along a south-facing fruit wall. "But my family has had
military connections for generations, back to the original baronies and
probably to Roman days. I could not fail my heritage, and I wasn't
about to let old Boney threaten all of this."

Boney's hopes of invading England had been dashed when
Nelson had dispatched the French fleet at Trafalgar in 1805. British
troops had not been dispatched to the Iberian Peninsula until several
years later, and I was still hazy regarding the precise motivation for
their deployment. Stopping the Corsican fiend had been the rhetoric
of the day, but regaining access to Continental markets had likely
been the true agenda.

Or perhaps, laying hold of French colonial riches had figured into
the equation.

I did not raise those questions with my escort, knowing how military men could wax lyrical about battles, campaigns, and marches.
My brother Felix had served, and from him, I'd gained a realistic and
ugly picture of warfare.

"Your wife has a military background, does she not?" I asked.

"Born in an officer's tent while her papa was on maneuvers,"
Rutland said, bending to snap off a fading daffodil and toss it into the
opposite lavender border. "Athena knows military history better than
Oxford dons know their Latin, and she's the equal of Wellington for
planning a campaign. I sometimes think she married me so she could
divert herself with the management of a hundred-odd inside servants
and another sixty out of doors. We did not expect you quite so early
in the day, and she will be mortified to have missed your arrival."

"The coach made good time," I replied. "For which providence
will doubtless exact a toll when we continue south."

"Then you must bide with us awhile and fortify yourself for the looming ordeal," Rutland said, his hand over mine on his arm. "We see little company here, except in high summer when the hillwalkers swarm the surrounds. They appear for a few weeks, like summer roses, and then decamp for the south for another year. We are always glad to see them arrive and equally glad to see them go."

"Are your neighbors sociable?" I asked as we turned the corner at the foot of the garden.

"Oh, very, and I have created a sort of old soldiers' regiment at the Wood as well. My erstwhile quartermaster, Thomas MacNeil, is my senior steward. Garth Jones, a former aide-de-camp, leases out the largest tenant property from us. Be warned: Athena will insist on taking you calling at Spruce Manor. I also employ Patrick O'Dea as my botanist and surveyor, another former aide-de-camp. We and our ladies form a very congenial company, and enlisted men who served under us have also found employment on the estate."

Rutland was proud of his congenial company, as if he'd carved out a circle of civilization in some foreign wilderness. Perhaps that instinct, to create a sense of home from a shared flask and stories around a campfire, was one of the military's strongest and best qualities.

"I very much appreciate your hospitality," I said as we passed a bed of yellow tulips. A lone red specimen bloomed near the center of the bed, which I found whimsical. Life was like that—unexpected at times, refusing to follow the ordained pattern. "No traveling coach appeals after about the third day on English roads."

"Excuse me," Rutland said, peeling free of my hand. "Somebody has been lax." He produced a penknife and sliced off the red tulip, pitching it into a hedge before I could claim it. "With six undergardeners and more than a dozen apprentices to oversee, discipline is sometimes wanting."

A horticultural staff that size would also be responsible for the kitchen gardens, apothecary garden, scent garden, and conservatory —on a large estate, much depended on the competence and diligence of the gardeners—but still... My father was an earl, and his seat was not nearly this impressive.

"We have been discovered," Rutland said, taking my arm again. "My darling wife approaches, and she will steal you away from me." He *twinkled* at me, as if he and I shared a luscious little secret, and then turned the same affable, boyish smile on the lady coming down the gravel walkway.

She was smiling as well, her skirts swishing as she marched along.

"You must be Lady Violet," she said. "Rutland, you are very naughty to whisk our guest off into the garden before she has been offered tea and a chance to refresh herself. My lady, good day. I would ask my husband to make the introductions, but we aren't particularly formal here at the Wood. I am Athena, Lady Rutland. My lord, be off with you. We ladies must get acquainted."

Clearly, I was in the presence of the general's daughter.

"I have my orders." Lord Rutland bowed to me and kissed his wife's cheek, though so casual was his aim that his lips grazed the corner of her mouth. She bore this affectionate display with good cheer—I had the sense her ladyship did everything with good cheer—and then took my arm with the same proprietary air her husband had displayed toward me.

"Come along, my lady. I have a tray on the way to the conservatory, and when we have drained the pot, we will find Monsieur St. Sevier and demand that he escort us on a tour of the house. You will meet the others at dinner, but I must have you to myself for a little while first."

Rutland beamed at me, saluted with two fingers, and strode off. Perhaps he enjoyed springing his wife on their guests, or perhaps the fault lay with St. Sevier, of the wistful smile.

In any case, Athena, Lady Rutland, was quite the most beautiful woman I had ever beheld.

CHAPTER TWO

"Please forgive my husband," Lady Rutland said, setting off down the garden path. "Rutland is an enthusiastic host, though he sometimes lacks sense. If you want to have a lie-down and some solitude, I will happily oblige you. Milly was hoping to meet you before supper tonight, though. Millicent, Mrs. Thomas MacNeil, our steward's wife, if we're to be precise. Milly and I are thick as thieves plotting to steal the crown jewels. I do hope you will join our larcenous circle while you bide at the Wood."

I tagged along, having little choice. In fact, I would have enjoyed some solitude, but I also wanted to know where St. Sevier would bide for the duration of our visit. Remaining attached to my hostess seemed the most expedient means of solving that riddle. Besides, I did not yet know where my own room was.

"Your husband is justifiably proud of his garden, and I needed to stretch my legs," I said, brushing my hand fleetingly over a raised lavender border. The scent soothed and refreshed, as this garden was meant to soothe and refresh.

"You are kind," Lady Rutland said, opening a tall gate in the south-facing wall. "But of course you are, for Hugh St. Sevier would only surround himself with kind, decent people. He was a great favorite in the army, and not only because of his impressive medical skills."

We approached a long, glass-roofed structure that ran parallel to the garden wall. In a former time, when the manor house itself had not yet reached its impressive dimensions, this might have been a stable block or row of cottages for the senior staff. The walls I could see were native stone, the trim painted white. Windows marched at regular intervals, suggesting stable doors from a bygone era.

"Our conservatory," Lady Rutland said, pushing open a door painted white. "The winters this far north are endless, and we must squeeze every ounce of summer we can from every beam of sunshine that graces us."

The ceiling and south-facing wall were glass, as were about half the side walls. Only the northern wall was made of stone. The space was in scale with everything else at the Wood—enormous—but lacked the ruthless order of the garden.

"In winter," Lady Rutland said, moving down a pathway of paving stones, "the conservatory is crowded more densely than a jungle. Moving the tender plants indoors takes several days and must be done according to a plan if we're to get it all sorted properly come spring. This time of year, we've started the reverse process."

She led me to the center of the building, a space fragrant with earth, greenery, and a hint of roses. A sort of parlor had been created by flanking a flagstone square with potted lemon and orange trees and arranging padded wicker furniture in the center. A sparrow flitted by, completing the sense of a secluded bower.

Lady Rutland took a seat in a wing chair and gestured me into the one next to her. If she had appeared lovely out of doors, the afternoon sun gilding her blond hair, the garden setting complementing cameo-perfect features, she was yet more stunning amid the greenery and grace of the conservatory.

English women hailing from the south tended to have blue eyes and blond hair. Her ladyship had not simply blond hair, but golden hair. I wanted to touch her coiffure to see if her locks were as silky as they appeared, though not a single curl violated the order of her chignon. If that was my reaction to her, what a sensation she must have created as the general's daughter among the young officers.

And her eyes were not blue, but rather, a soft, emerald green fringed with lashes darker than her hair. Her gaze was knowing, kind, and patient, with a hint of rueful humor buried in the depths. She was no girl asserting her wiles to encourage flirtation, she was a woman who'd seen much and had the wisdom not to be impressed with her own appearance.

Everything about her begged to be immortalized in good portraiture, from her graceful height to her generous womanly curves to pale hands that many a lieutenant had doubtless composed odes to.

I should have hated her. I was of medium-shortish height and had *lamentably* brown hair and unremarkable blue eyes. My figure was a trifle embonpoint, in my opinion, and yet, I hoped I had not yet passed into the euphemistic territory encompassed by the term *matronly*.

Please, not so soon, and without any children to give the appellation warmth.

"Tell me how you and St. Sevier met," Lady Rutland said, holding out a tray of shortbread to me.

"Socially." I took a small piece and helped myself to a plate glazed with songbirds and blooming morning glory vines. "I emerged from mourning by attending musicales. One can leave at the interval, easily avoid unpleasant company, skip the buffet, and sometimes hear good music. St. Sevier was escorting a cousin who was performing a Beethoven slow movement. We had had a previous passing acquaintance, nothing of substance."

The memory was a little personal, and not entirely sweet.

"Monsieur shows to good advantage in formal attire," Lady Rutland said, removing the linen swaddling the teapot. "Always did. Englishmen love their dashing uniforms, while Frenchmen prefer *fashion* even within the confines of a uniform. Their art is subtle and intriguing. Did you and he strike up a conversation about French versus Italian opera?"

I would not have been knowledgeable about such a topic, though doubtless, the general's daughter was.

"I fell asleep on his shoulder."

Her ladyship looked up from pouring two cups of tea. "Fell asleep on his shoulder? Lady Violet, how original. I like that. Bold and unassuming all at once. You fell asleep on his shoulder. Well done, I say. St. Sevier was never one to pursue a lady, but he could hardly ignore one sleeping on his very person. Tell me what happened next."

I had never shared this story and did not want to disclose it now. Nonetheless, her ladyship's air invited confidences amid all good cheer, and I was abruptly famished. I bit off half the shortbread and chose my words.

"Mourning had disturbed the rhythm of my days and nights," I said. "After two years of what amounted to house arrest, I was both anxious to go out and loath to do so. I was tired, but could not sleep. I wanted to be with people pursuing entertainments free of grieving rituals, even though the whole business of socializing felt pointless to me."

"How do you take your tea?"

"A drop of honey will do and a dash of cream." When private, I had been known to indulge in more than a drop and a dash, but this was an interrogation, however friendly. Time to indulge later.

"So you fell exhausted on St. Sevier's person between the movements of a dance suite?"

"I was felled by the Beethoven slow movement in a slow triple meter. All dark and mournful, but profoundly peaceful too. St. Sevier indulged me, apparently, for I don't recall more than the exposition of the first theme." I recalled Hugh's scent, a soft hint of honeysuckle, and his mellifluous accent, and the sheer pleasure of long-denied human closeness. When applause woke me, Hugh ignored my great lapse and asked to accompany me to the buffet.

"He was gallant, I'll wager," her ladyship said, sipping at a plain cup of stout China black. "On campaign, we do not subject widows to two years of cowering at home, where they weep into their late husband's nightshirt. Among the lower ranks, a widow was on campaign often remarried within a fortnight of being bereaved."

Was that announcement intended to shock me? I thought not, but rather to cast judgment on mourning processes that served some purposes while thwarting others of equal value.

"Remarried within a fortnight?" I asked. "That's not an exaggeration?"

"Not at all. Life at war is an odd combination of strict protocol and ruthless pragmatism. There are rules about whether and how officers marry, how many wives can accompany a regiment, and so forth. Outside the rules, women live a precarious existence. The army needed women on the Peninsula, as cooks, laundresses, seamstresses, and..." She waved a hand, indicating another profession of lesser repute and longer provenance than the aforesaid.

"So the army needed women but failed to respect them?"

Her ladyship dunked a piece of shortbread in her tea. "Why should the army be any different from the rest of society? Your London neighbors did not want to be afflicted with the sight of your grief, so you wore weeds and a veil, remained at home, and avoided socializing. Fine for the neighbors, but I gather you fared poorly under those strictures."

I had honestly fared poorly as a wife too. "Tell me more about regimental marriage." I ought to have posed a question rather than issued an order, but such was Lady Rutland's influence that issuing a command struck me as the better choice. Then too, I was prey to an unbecoming desire to know how Hugh and his Annie had come to be man and wife.

"From the perspective of the infantrymen," Lady Rutland said, "women had it easy. The ladies were not expected to fight—though they occasionally did—they were provided for, they enjoyed all the camaraderie and informality of camp life, and their contributions were valued. Moreover, most of them had a power of choice they enjoyed nowhere else in society, simply as a result of scarcity."

The tea was hot, a small miracle given how far we were from the manor's kitchens, and the shortbread fresh. The conversation was also interesting, and yet, I was nagged by a need to know where Hugh St. Sevier was and what he was up to.

"Did the women enjoy this sanguine view of their own circumstances?"

Green eyes turned pensive. "A lady can't know when she follows the drum exactly what that entails. Then her husband is killed in some stupid ambush, and there she is, a widow, far from home, and the military will not bother to send her back to England. The army paid her spouse poorly, and he probably drank what coin he earned. She has little means of supporting herself anywhere but in camp, and men are literally lining up for a chance to take her to wife. I know of circumstances where soldiers diced to decide which of them would solve a widow's lack of husband."

And our gallant officers had not intervened in such goings-on? "Pragmatic, as you say." Also barbaric, but then, the business of the military was war.

"Many an English wife was stranded in France when peace was declared, Lady Violet. If she wasn't on the regimental rolls, a husband's charity was her only hope of returning home. France had been devastated by its own army, and remaining behind was not... not a happy fate."

This was an aspect of military service I had not asked St. Sevier or my brother Felix about: What of the women? English armies marched, and women marched with them. If I were to ask anybody such questions, I'd put them to Sebastian MacHeath, Lord Dunkeld. Sebastian could be as brusque as any Scotsman, and he had never coddled me.

"And yet, you married a soldier," I said, "one of considerable rank. Why?"

Perfectly arched brows drew down. "Because Damien spoke so

lovingly of his home. He was a younger son dispatched to the military in the usual fashion, and his older brother was consumptive. Damien longed to return home, as a steward, as second-in-command, as heir presumptive, as anything, provided he could spend the rest of his days at the Wood."

In addition to having a legacy of great wealth, Damien was also charming and attractive. A shrewd choice for a woman bent on escaping the military.

I was spared a polite rejoinder by footsteps coming up the walkway.

"There you are," a lady called out, emerging through the greenery. "I am late to the party as usual, but I see some shortbread yet remains. You must be Lady Violet. I'm Milly MacNeil, and I thank you most sincerely for hauling Hugh St. Sevier into our midst. His dancing alone endears him to any lady with two feet."

She smiled and winked, behavior I would never have encountered from a new acquaintance in a London drawing room.

But then, Milly MacNeil, red-haired, merry, and buxom, was, if anything, even more lovely than Athena, Lady Rutland. Women that attractive could bend rules and be pronounced original, while lesser ladies fretted over what color gloves to wear to a ridotto.

I rose and curtseyed. "Mrs. MacNeil, a pleasure to make your acquaintance. St. Sevier speaks very highly of your husband."

"Don't believe a word of it," Milly said, taking a small sofa on the other side of the low table. "You will meet my darling Tommie at supper tonight, and because God shows no mercy to a lady's toes, you might have to dance with him before you withdraw to the south. What is this I hear about your acquaintance with Colonel Sebastian MacHeath? Our favorite Scot has gone for a marquess, and we are all dying to know how he's bearing up. And you are Felix Deerfield's sister, if I read Debrett's correctly—which I do. Tell us of our delightful Felix. Athena, be a love and pour a woman a spot of tea. Interrogating guests is thirsty work."

She grinned at me again, and I smiled back, for once grateful for all the years I'd spent on campaign myself across the ballrooms and battlefields of Mayfair.

~

"Did Athena put you on the rack?" St. Sevier asked, passing me a tot of brandy.

I took a sip for medicinal reasons, then set my glass aside. "Tea with the ladies was an interview, to say the least. What of you? Did you explore the library?"

"I did, but Rutland has been culling the collection, and I found little in the way of interesting old pamphlets. I confess I got to wandering." St. Sevier held his arms open. "Come here, Violet."

Had his demand not been softened with a smile and a particular tilt to his head, I would have ignored him for form's sake. Instead, I went into his embrace, pathetically grateful to be held, though not sure why that should be.

"I fretted," I said, burrowing closer. "I saw the pretty housekeeper lead you away, and I fretted. 'Where is he going?' 'When will I see him again?' I hate that."

St. Sevier stroked my back, and if I loved nothing else about the man, I loved his touch. He could convey calm in a few gentle caresses, and I badly needed calming.

"I had no idea Rutland Wood was such a palace," he said. "You are overwhelmed?"

"Not quite overwhelmed, and it's not the house that bothers me, or not strictly the house." I eased away when I wanted to cling. "My first foray from London after I put off mourning was a house party where I knew most of the guests and wasn't that far from home. The second was to my family seat, where I know everybody. The third was to Scotland, to see one old friend and pay calls on another."

St. Sevier poured himself a drink, a mundane little task that I loved watching him perform. He was elegant in his bones, whether wearing formal attire or lounging about as God made him. I liked simply looking at Hugh. I liked hearing his accented voice. I liked touching him.

This degree of attraction was new to me and a source of both glee and anxiety. What was treasured could be taken away.

"Now," he said, facing me and bracing his hips against the sideboard, "you are in strange surrounds, where you know nobody but my humble self."

I retrieved my drink and considered his words. "It's worse than that. I know you to some extent, but *they* know you in ways I do not. These people shared a whole life with you, one where widows remarried within a fortnight of losing a spouse and were then left behind when they became unnecessary ballast. Rutland and his lady have been to war with you."

And why had Lady Rutland made it a priority to emphasize to me all I did not share with my own escort?

"They have been to war with me, true, while you have been to bed with me. Are you growing possessive, Violet? A bit jealous, perhaps?" He sounded curious and a little hopeful.

"I have been made aware of how little you and I truly know of each other. I would not have coped well with camp life, St. Sevier."

He pushed away from the sideboard. "Come, I will show you something to make you smile." He took my hand and led me to a set of French doors. "The housekeeper put us in the family wing, which means the arrangements are not as formal as they would be in a guest wing."

I stepped out onto a balcony that overlooked paddocks at the foot of a pine-clad hill. Horses grazed contently on spring grass, and a pair of chestnut foals cavorted in the late afternoon sun. But for the dark pines looming over the whole, this was rural England at her bucolic best.

"Very pretty," I said. "My room enjoys the same view."

He turned me gently to the left. "Our sitting rooms share a balcony, *mon coeur*. We also face away from the back gardens, meaning any comings and goings on our balcony will not be observed from our host and hostess's apartment. MacNeil and his wife bide at the back of the first floor, so we are safe from their scrutiny as well."

The garden would be visible from the far corner of St. Sevier's balcony and from his bedroom windows, but the balcony paralleled the side of the house, not the back.

"You didn't wander. You scouted the terrain." Something I typically did whenever I arrived to a new venue. "Thank you."

"We will wander together tomorrow morning," St. Sevier said, "and then you will worry a little less. Rutland Wood appears no different from many other English domestic monstrosities. A harmless little hunting box or farmhouse became the object of some successful family's vanity. Wings were added, additions put on, outbuildings erected, until a serviceable home became a series of linked exhibition halls."

"And then the family beggars itself trying to keep its exhibition halls heated. I need to know one thing before we change for dinner, St. Sevier."

He dropped my hand. "You want to know if I was intimate with Lady Rutland or Millicent MacNeil?"

"Or with any woman I will meet while we bide here."

St. Sevier gazed out over the lush paddocks, drink in his hand. The picture he made was breathtakingly handsome. He would have been equally attractive as a younger man.

"Will you promise to be jealous if I bedded them both, Violet?"

Yes. I would also be angry, because St. Sevier had led me into this situation without warning me before I'd made the decision to allow our sortie to the Lakes. Gentlemanly discretion and convenient deception could be twins all too easily.

"If I know the history," I said, "I will be better able to weather the innuendo and casual sniping. Freddie was scrupulous about keeping his hands off my social acquaintances, one of few considerations he felt he owed his wife." In Freddie's own words, the ensuing drama would have put Drury Lane out of business.

I hadn't argued with him, but by that point in our marriage, there would have been little drama. Only more disappointment.

"You must understand, Violet, that I was a Frenchman in the English military community. Any woman consorting with me would have been suspect, as I was suspect. For a general's daughter or an officer's wife to flirt with me was acceptable—everybody flirted with everybody—but my purpose was medical, not social."

"So these women were not your lovers?"

He ran a hand through his hair, sighed the universal sigh of the beleaguered male, and shook his head.

"I was never intimate with Millicent or Athena. I will claim a similar innocence where Mrs. O'Dea and Mrs. Jones are concerned, for you will doubtless meet them while we bide here. I was not one of *their kind*, in many ways, and I kept to my place."

I looped my arm through his and leaned against him. I had come close to offending Gallic pride and owed St. Sevier amends.

"I am not *their kind* either," I said. "It's as if the ladies are still on campaign somehow. Eschewing etiquette, assuming a familiarity they have not earned, singing the praises of army life in all its brutality. I'm to call Lady Rutland by her given name and Mrs. MacNeil by her nickname. They referred to Felix by name rather than by his rank and asked after Dunkeld as if he were a boy off at public school."

"That bothers you?"

"Disconcerts me. I am easily disconcerted apparently."

St. Sevier wrapped his arm around my shoulders and kissed my cheek. "A year ago, you were still in weeds, dreading divine services, and unwilling to leave your house even to call on family. Now you racket about Britain, have a handsome and devoted lover, and embroil yourself in intrigues involving missing bridegrooms and purloined jewelry. A little fretting is permitted, Violet."

How I loved him. "Thank you. I am a ninnyhammer."

He held his glass to my lips, and I took another sip, though the brandy was nothing remarkable.

"Your maid will be waiting for you," he said, "and I must make myself presentable as well. Rutland is doubtless punctual about meals."

"I want to like him, but he's charming, and I am by nature suspicious of charm." I wasn't too keen on men who tossed aside innocent red tulips either.

St. Sevier eased away. "One has sensed your wariness where charm is concerned, oddly enough. Rutland was a good commanding officer, Violet. He listened to me when I told him the latrines had to be downhill from any water supplies and the mess hall uphill from the living quarters. He took the welfare of his men seriously when not all of his ilk did."

I preceded St. Sevier into the sitting room. "I would like to hear more about your army days, when you are inclined to tell the tale."

"You will hear many a tale at supper," he said, returning his glass to the sideboard. "The stories will all be humorous. I will laugh appropriately and maybe even tell an anecdote or two of my own."

"But?"

For a moment, his eyes looked haunted. "But I hate fog because it puts me in mind of the blinding smoke of a battlefield. Some marching songs bring back nightmares. I hope one day to develop a medical practice as an accoucheur because I never again want to deal in the matters familiar to a battlefield surgeon. The sound of thunder still unnerves me. You will think me a ninnyhammer."

I hugged him, hard. "I think you miraculous." I slipped out the door before allowing him to see that his recitation had moved me to tears.

CHAPTER THREE

My maid, Lucy Hewitt, had taken the measure of Rutland Wood from belowstairs and dressed me accordingly. She insisted I wear a short-sleeved lavender silk evening gown—the shade was widowed, as she said, but not *too* widowed. My slippers were mulberry, my shawl peacock green and blue, my jewels amethysts. I hadn't worn such finery in years and felt more than a little conspicuous, particularly because Lucy denied me the modesty of a fichu.

"You'll have a shawl, my lady," she said, threading a bouquet of silk violets into my chignon. "You also have a bosom most women would envy. Hold still."

"How has your reception been among the staff?" I asked.

"There's a mob of them, though they are friendly enough. Three senior footmen, at least two dozen more below them, and a first footman organizing the lot. A butler and two underbutlers. Maids by the score, three undercooks, a half-dozen scullery maids, three potboys, an assistant steward just for the pantries and wine cellar... Half of 'em are mustered-out military, or they followed the drum for a sweetheart." She stood back and eyed her handiwork. "You'll do, my lady. Come have a look."

I rose from the vanity stool and accepted the shawl Lucy handed me. The woman reflected in the cheval mirror was possessed of some dignity and a certain quiet attractiveness. In the lavender dress, I was neither showy nor retiring, and the simple lines flowing from an old-fashioned *empire* bodice flattered my endowments.

Perhaps the word I was looking for was *poised*. The Lady Violet whom Lucy had created was poised and calm. "You have worked wonders," I said, draping the shawl around my shoulders.

"Not like that." Lucy arranged the fabric like a stole rather than a shawl so my entire décolletage was covered, and my dress was visible from the ribs down. "Then you take it off at supper, and the gentlemen ogle you in earnest between courses."

"How do you know these things?" I asked, turning slightly and using the mirror to admire the effect of her subtle alteration.

"I'm not pretty like some," Lucy replied. "I have to be clever. Mind you don't be late. Lord Rutland is apparently a stickler for the clock."

"You needn't wait up for me, Lucy. Find some supper, and I'll see you in the morning."

"I could take the cot in the dressing closet, my lady. I've my own room off the maids' dormitory. Doesn't feel quite proper to sleep all on my lonesome."

"Enjoy a little privacy," I said, knowing it was my own privacy I sought to protect, for all that I trusted Lucy's discretion utterly. "You are lady's maid to the Earl of Derwent's only daughter, and for all its size, Rutland Wood is home to a mere barony. And one more thing, Lucy."

"Ma'am?"

"You are quite pretty. Mr. Upjohn would agree with me." Rhys Upjohn was valet to the Marquess of Dunkeld and something of a favorite with Lucy.

I left her smiling as she finished unpacking my trunks.

Rutland Wood manor was laid out as an L. One wing housed the family apartments and the public rooms. The other included a semi-sunken ballroom and gallery. That half of the house also included estate offices and an old-fashioned armory housing the family archives, as well as some quarters for the junior staff. Barracks, to use the term Lady Rutland had applied when explaining the layout of the house to me.

The kitchens were centered belowstairs at the intersection of the two wings, with pantries, cellars, herbal, servants' hall, and senior staff apartments branching off from them.

My route to the first formal parlor required a detour to the ballroom wing if I was to avoid the drafty main staircase—besides, I wanted to explore a bit, the better to orient myself. I had five minutes to traverse a good distance, as best I could grasp the layout of the house, so I was moving smartly along when raised voices caused me to slow my steps. Two men were having a proper row behind a half-closed door. I recognized Lord Rutland's voice, clipped and exasperated—no charm *at all*—while the man answering him had the very same Perthshire burr I'd enjoyed so thoroughly in Scotland.

I did not need to eavesdrop per se to hear the Scotsman expostulate about *damned tulips* and Lord Rutland's rejoinder referencing *undisciplined laggards*. Could this entire altercation be over the errant red tulip his lordship had found amid a bed of yellow blooms?

I had four brothers and a father much enamored of his own consequence. The male of the species, in my experience, could create enough drama *to put Drury Lane out of business* every bit as easily as could the female. Whatever the cause of the disagreement, it was none of my affair.

I hurried along, stopping to steady myself only as I approached the first formal parlor. I was the daughter of an earl, a woman of mature years with consider experience navigating polite social gatherings. I was still silently lecturing myself about the depths of my confidence and sophistication when a tall man in evening attire approached me from the direction of the main staircase.

"You must be Lady Violet," he said in a beguilingly soft brogue. "Patrick O'Dea at your service, if you will forgive my forwardness."

He bowed, and I curtseyed, though I could have done with St. Sevier's steadying arm. Lady Rutland and Mrs. MacNeil were stunningly attractive women. Lord Rutland was a handsome and charming man, and Patrick O'Dea was as beautiful as a fellow could be while still embodying every masculine ideal.

His eyes were blue, his hair sable, and his brows a trifle heavy. Perhaps his looks were a cross between the dark coloring of the Picts and the generous stature of the Vikings, or maybe a swashbuckling Iberian lurked a few branches higher on his family tree. His jaw was square and had the Creator stopped there, Patrick O'Dea would have been merely attractive on a grand scale.

But the Deity had been in a lavish mood when fashioning Mr. O'Dea, imbuing him with cheekbones worthy of Byron's most dashing Corsair and a full, smiling mouth that cast the Corsair's moody demeanor quite in the shade.

The final touch that made Mr. O'Dea's impact truly memorable was the warmth and humor in his eyes. His smile said he did not precisely know how these great good looks had befallen him, and nobody ought to be very impressed by them, for *he* certainly wasn't.

"Shall we lurk out here until the last possible moment?" he asked. "Jones and MacNeil will be jealous that I got to meet you before they did, as will my lady wife."

"We shall go in, lest we be late for inspection. I'm told Lord Rutland values punctuality."

Mr. O'Dea winged his arm, and I took it. "Rutland doesn't merely value punctuality, he regards it as a cardinal virtue, the sine qua non of good society, the achievement without which Saint Peter will not grant admittance to the celestial realm, be ye ever so pure a soul otherwise. You can take the man out of the military, but seldom the reverse. The army would be in complete disarray without its schedules."

We entered the parlor to find St. Sevier flanked by Lady Rutland and Millicent MacNeil. Two other women were in conversation with a spare, elegantly mustached fellow of just over medium height. I looked from him to the women—Mrs. O'Dea and Mrs. Jones, no doubt—and resigned myself to being the wren among the peacocks.

These people were gorgeous, every one of them, each in a different way. I could never be gorgeous, but when St. Sevier bowed over my hand and escorted me through the introductions, I managed to at least keep hold of my poise.

As events unfolded over the next fortnight, I would lose my grip on even that modest asset, but when the rest of the guests assembled, I chatted, I smiled, I sipped my wine, and I counted the minutes until I could retire to my own room, or better still, to St. Sevier's.

"I liked Mr. MacNeil," I said, sinking onto a sofa in St. Sevier's sitting room. "He had no need to talk for the sake of grabbing his share of the conversation." Then too, Thomas MacNeil, senior steward at the Wood and Millicent's spouse, was also merely handsome rather than stunning.

That alone endeared him to me.

Like his wife, he had red hair, though more auburn than flaming orange. Unlike Millicent, Thomas MacNeil was quiet. He spoke quietly, he moved quietly, at least at dinner. Arguing with his employer, he was apparently less reticent.

"You have a soft spot for the Scots," St. Sevier said, coming down beside me. "I grew to like them very much when I was studying medicine in Edinburgh. I grew to respect them on the battlefield. Shall you have a nightcap?"

"No, thank you, but help yourself." The wine at dinner had been plentiful, though honestly not that appealing. I eased off my slippers and curled my legs under me. "Were the stories true?"

Men sewing others' tents closed, hiding one another's boots the morning before inspection, and generally behaving like public-school boys rather than a deadly fighting force.

"For the most part."

"Not the whole truth?"

"The business of an army on the march is war. There was merriment, also the occasional summary execution, brutal floggings for insignificant infractions, petty dramas of every description, disease, maimings, and always—*always*—death."

Silliness and violence, gallantry and tragedy. I felt a need to change the subject, not for myself—I was vulgarly curious to know more—but for Hugh, who had volunteered for years of military life all for the purpose of alleviating suffering and reducing the death toll.

"I head Lord Rutland and Mr. MacNeil arguing," I said. "Right before dinner. They were all smiles in the parlor, but going at it a few minutes before."

St. Sevier leaned his head back against the cushions and closed his eyes. "Commanding officers like to give orders, and they like even better when their orders are followed to the letter. I suspect some of them like best of all when their orders are *not* obeyed, for then the senior officer can comport himself like the wrath of Jehovah."

I shifted to straddle Hugh's lap and set about undoing his cravat. The pin nestled among the linen and lace was amber, a fine, understated complement to his brown eyes.

"I sensed tension between the ladies," I said, drawing the neckcloth free and draping it over the back of the sofa. "Lady Rutland and Mrs. MacNeil are in accord, while Mrs. O'Dea and Mrs. Jones are also allies, but the four of them together are not entirely harmonious."

"I don't know Mrs. O'Dea that well. Mrs. Jones spent a lot of time in my surgery, and for that alone I will hear nothing said against her. Some women will sit by a soldier's cot and kindly read him the Twenty-third Psalm while he expires. Daphne Jones would see that no man was left to lie in his own filth, no man allowed to thirst in vain. She was tireless and didn't care if a fellow was French, English, German, or American."

Nursing the ill was considered a lady's responsibility in her own household, and a less than proper profession otherwise, for the reason St. Sevier had just described. Even more than the barber-surgeon, the nurse dealt with the ailing body in all its lowly realities. That she eased suffering and saved lives wasn't enough to redeem her from censure.

"Mrs. Jones is quite the proper lady now," I said. "I'm to call on her at Spruce Manor tomorrow with Lady Rutland and Mrs. O'Dea."

"Tomorrow afternoon, perhaps," St. Sevier said, urging me against him. "Tomorrow morning, you and I go for a stroll, madam. We find peace and quiet and pretend to read poetry to one another."

"You are undoing my dress."

"A thankless business, but I am ever willing to be useful. What do you suppose Rutland and MacNeil were arguing about?"

I closed my eyes as St. Sevier worked his way down the hooks at the back of my dress. "I did not want to be late for supper, so I hurried past, but it appeared they argued about flowers. Tulips, to be specific."

"Of which the estate boasts thousands. Shall you leave your necklace on?"

Jewelry in bed struck me as silly, an affectation for odalisques. "No, thank you."

St. Sevier soon had my dress undone, and rather than fall sleep on his shoulder, I rose and preceded him into the bedroom. He followed, and it occurred to me that since we'd left the company, his loverly advances had been of the understated variety.

"You are preoccupied," I said, unbuttoning his waistcoat and shirt. "Also probably tired."

"I have not seen these people in years and have few good memories of the time I spent with them. Being among them... I had not thought to find their company disconcerting, and yet, it is."

I pushed Hugh's jacket off his shoulders and hung it in the cedar-lined wardrobe. His waistcoat came next, then his sleeve buttons. I had undressed my late husband any number of times, but the process had been perfunctory, not a gradual peeling away of the day's cares and frustrations.

"I did not go to war with them," I said, sitting on the step beside the bed and lifting my skirts, "and I find their company disconcerting. They are all still somehow marching in lockstep, and yet, one senses undercurrents too." I untied my garters and rolled down my stockings.

When I looked up, Hugh was leaning on the bedpost, watching me. "I might be poor company tonight, Violet."

"If that means you are not inclined to ravish me, be at ease. I am not particularly in the mood to be ravished. Shall I leave you to battle the nightmares on your own?"

He approached and gathered me close so that my cheek was pressed to his flat belly. "I might thrash about and yell profanities in my sleep, though I'm told they are always French profanities. I once gave Annie quite the bruise on her arm. I struck her with *mon coude...* my elbow."

When Hugh's command of English slipped, he was either exhausted or upset. I suspected he was both.

"I will be sure to avoid any flailing *coudes,* and your paltry cursing will be as nothing to a woman with four brothers. Between them all, they stumble around in at least eight languages." I patted Hugh's bum. "Not counting dog Latin."

He kissed the top of my head. "*Je t'adore, mon coeur.*"

We had settled into a pattern in Scotland—turning down the covers, using the warmer, taking turns behind the privacy screen, banking the fire. I hoped the routine soothed some of Hugh's upset, as it quelled my own uneasiness with a day more challenging than I'd anticipated. When Hugh hung his dressing gown on the bedpost and climbed in beside me, I curled up next to him.

"You miss Annie," I said, for surely memories of her had also been stirred by today's events.

Hugh looped an arm around my shoulders. "God spare me from perceptive Englishwomen."

I cuddled closer and took his hand, resigning myself to patience. "And yet, you do miss her."

"Annie and I had settled into bitter silence," Hugh said, "by the time she decided to make her way to the coast. I would have tried to talk her out of leaving had I known of her plans, but I also understand why she left. There was no reasoning with her, of course, and she was not wrong to leave. We were not *compatible*, not *amiable*," he said, giving the words their French pronunciations. "But I would have wished her well, would have offered her my wages, my knife, my cloak... something. She took my name and got mostly bad memories for her trouble. Nothing more, and... *Je suis hanté*."

Freddie haunted me, though less so the longer I was widowed. I had not understood him, had not had a frame of reference for sorting out a man who was both happily and regularly debauched and a loyal and generous spouse. Not faithful, though—never that—and increasingly unhappy with my unwillingness to bend to his version of marital accord.

"You never said good-bye," I murmured. "You never had the chance. Perhaps it's good that you came here, Hugh. By bringing her memory closer, you might be more at peace with your loss."

To my surprise, his reply was to shift himself over me and commence a spate of tender kisses. For a man who had proclaimed himself possibly poor company, he treated me to a loving that was sweet, slow, and somehow sad for us both, also fortifying.

I thought he had fallen asleep in my arms, a comforting weight of replete lover at peace for the nonce, when he spoke quietly.

"You mentioned that these people know me and went to war with me, and that you and I are of only recent acquaintance."

"Recent, but treasured, acquaintance," I said. "I no longer envy your military friends the duration of their acquaintance as I did earlier in the day."

"And yet,"—he rolled away, keeping hold of my hand—"you made a valid point. They knew me when I was wed to Annie, when I was new to the practice of medicine, when I yet had brothers extant. MacNeil was my best man."

I hoped that day at least was a sweet memory for all concerned.

"And they knew you when you got word Annie had been killed by a French patrol."

Hugh turned away, onto his side, and as I spooned myself around him, he kissed my knuckles and wrapped my arm about his waist.

"Sebastian MacHeath knew you years ago, Violet." Hugh's words were quiet, almost bleak. "Your marquess knows your past and is well acquainted with the family you sprang from. He was an innocent with you in a way I will never be. I envy him that."

That St. Sevier would admit to envy—and of Sebastian?—was extraordinary, but also a means of telling me he understood my consternation regarding his military connections.

"What matters to me now," I said, "is the man who has asked for the privilege of sharing my future and with whom I share my bed. Go to sleep, St. Sevier, and if any patrols come by, they will have to get past me before they can haunt you."

As it happened, we slept peacefully through the night. When I stole into my own room at first light, I did so with a sense of having grown closer to my lover. Hugh and I were not innocents coming to first love with stars in our eyes, nor did I want us to be.

I'd married with stars in my eyes, and Hugh had gone off to war with stars in his, and just look how those ventures had turned out.

"The staff takes meals in assigned shifts," Lucy said as I settled onto the vanity stool. "The lot of them sit at assigned tables, like in a mess hall. Parlormaids do not sit with scullery maids. The seamstresses share a table with the senior chambermaids. God forbid a footman should long to dine next to his sister."

"Or his sweetheart?" I rejoined.

Lucy began undoing my braid. "I suppose that's what the pantries are for. Lord knows they go on for miles. I much preferred Derwent Hall myself."

I was more familiar with my maid than a proper widow ought to

be and found Lucy's tendency to prattle first thing in the day soothing. She had been through mourning with me and had imposed a
basic routine on my days that had preserved my sanity when that
item had been imperiled. She had joined forces with St. Sevier to
urge me to attend my first house party following second mourning,
and I considered her an ally.

If not always diplomatic in her loyalty.

"Derwent Hall is a more modest estate, Lucy." My father was
also not of a military bent. He ruled by charm, guile, and tradition as
much as by the authority of his earldom.

"Size got nothing to do with it," Lucy retorted, setting aside my
hair ribbon. "At Derwent Hall, everybody knows where to sit without
being told, and everybody eats together. The bootboy hears the
undercoachman's tales from Town. The whole table gets the gossip
the undercook brings home from market. Derwent Hall's people are
not divided up by rank at each meal. They know their places and also
know they are valued."

"Even Derwent Hall sets a second table." The upper servants sat
at that table, as well as any visiting artisans or tradesmen of insuffi-
cient rank to break bread with the earl's family. A lady's companion
would eat with the family, a senior law clerk bringing documents out
from Town would eat at the second table.

"Derwent Hall sets a second table for Sunday supper and on
special occasions, but never at breakfast or nooning. You will pay a
call today,' Lucy said, eyeing my hair. "Shall we go a bit fancy?"

"First, I will stroll the grounds with Monsieur St. Sevier, so
nothing fancy. A coronet will do." Besides, I did not want to provoke
a competition for who could be the finest lady at the Wood, a competition I would lose, despite my social standing. "How do you know I'll
pay a call?"

Lucy undid my braid and wielded the brush in efficient strokes.
When St. Sevier brushed out my hair, the effect was far more restful.

"I took my evening meal at the same table as the lady's maids for
Lady Rutland, Mrs. MacNeil, Mrs. O'Dea, and Mrs. Jones. You will

call on Mrs. Jones at Spruce Manor today, and tomorrow Mrs. O'Dea will take you on a walking tour of the estate. She's married to the botanist-surveyor Irish fella. They dwell in their own cottage."

An entire table of lady's maids struck me as more peril to the king's peace than all the flirting footmen in Cumbria.

"Lucy, please do not engage in gossip."

She finished the first braid and tied it off with a blue ribbon. "I would never. I buttered my bread and talked of the weather."

Lucy had affixed my braids atop my head in a demure coronet before a question occurred to me. "Why would the lady's maids even be here last night? The party gathered for dinner, not a formal ball." A lady's maid might accompany her employer to a grand affair, the better to touch up a coiffure or deal with a torn hem, but not to an informal dinner.

"When the four couples get together, the guests all apparently spend the night at the Wood. Saves pouring the Irishman and the Welshman into coaches as the moon sets, I suppose, and Lord knows there's room for a regiment of guests here. They form a regular company on Sundays, I take it, and on certain other occasions."

"Country life can be congenial." Also gossipy, lonely, and tedious. I nonetheless appreciated the warning that I might have more than my host and hostess and the MacNeils to contend with at breakfast. Patrick O'Dea had struck me as particularly garrulous at supper, and I wasn't up to hearing more tales of army life first thing in the day.

"You'll want a real shawl," Lucy said, opening my wardrobe. "Mornings are nippy hereabouts. If you take the maids' stairs down the corridor, you end up just outside the library, and the breakfast parlor is three doors up on the other side of the foyer."

I understood those directions, having a capacity for mentally mapping my surrounds. I would fill in more of that map as St. Sevier and I conducted our reconnaissance mission. I wrapped the shawl about myself, grateful for its warmth, and accepted the flat straw hat Lucy thrust into my hands.

"They like Monsieur," she said, passing me cotton gloves to match the cream wool shawl. "Belowstairs. The first underbutler said civilian life looks like it agrees with the Frenchie doctor."

"How could an underbutler know such a thing?"

"Simmons was a batman or drill sergeant or some such. Said Monsieur cast the English surgeons into the shade, and all the men asked for him if they got injured. The ladies had need of him, too, when a lying-in turned difficult. Didn't matter if she was a laundress or the general's wife. He did what he could."

While his own young wife had grown estranged and difficult. "Monsieur's healing vocation is sincere."

"Too bad he's so hard on the eyes, eh?" Lucy grinned and set about making the bed. "They noticed that, too, those fancy lady's maids. I don't care what table you're assigned to, human nature makes us more alike than different."

"I cannot argue the point, as I am too hungry to think clearly. I'll see you before dinner."

I left her thwacking pillows and humming, suggesting Simmons or some other lucky fellow had caught Lucy's eye. As long as she was discreet about her pleasures, I considered them no business of mine.

St. Sevier, looking scrumptious in riding attire, met me at the door to my sitting room. "You've been out for a hack?" I asked.

"I have." He kissed my cheek, a Continental presumption I quite adored. "You abandoned me, and I could not get back to sleep for remembering the night's glories. Shall we to breakfast?"

He was once again on his mettle, which reassured me. I should not need reassurance. I was an honored guest at a gracious manor full of friendly people pleased to make my acquaintance. I was also apparently still something of a ninnyhammer about unfamiliar surroundings, an affliction that hadn't been as much in evidence in Scotland.

"Lucy says the maids' stairs are the most direct route." I took St. Sevier's arm for the pleasure of the familiarity. "My belly is telling me to avoid the more circuitous route."

"My heart is telling me we might linger for a moment on the maids' stairs."

"That suggestion comes from someplace other than your heart."

We bantered our way down the corridor until we came to the discreet panel masking the door to the stairway designated for female staff. I opened the door rather than wait for St. Sevier to perform that courtesy and was surprised to hear a male voice.

"You know I'm right, Milly mine." Patrick O'Dea's soft brogue drifted up the steps on a wheedling note.

I drew back, leaving the door cracked. On the landing a few steps down, Patrick O'Dea and Millicent MacNeil were in an embrace too close to qualify as friendly. She was in a morning gown and heavy wool shawl, her hair in a thick copper braid down the middle of her back. His attire lacked a coat, and he had yet to shave.

He had one shoulder braced against the wall and one hand on Millicent's waist. His spine was relaxed, his hips canted at an attitude that suggested erotic invitation.

"You always think you're right," Millicent replied, smoothing her hand over his chest. "That's the trouble. You *all* always think you're right." She turned away, and O'Dea caught her by the hand.

"I'm of the lowliest rank in this company," he said, "but if you ladies speak up, you'll be listened to."

"Have you mentioned your bright idea to Kathleen?" Millicent's posture as she posed that question was half coy, half resisting. She did not shake free of O'Dea's grasp, though she remained half facing away.

"I first seek the support of the most sensible of the ladies."

St. Sevier touched my shoulder. He was frowning, and for good reason. This was not a conversation anybody should overhear. I closed the door quietly.

"What do you suppose his 'bright idea' concerns?" I asked as we retraced our steps and made for the main foyer.

"You will not speculate, Violet. You will not conjecture. Above all things, you will not *investigate*. We are spending a pleasant fortnight among my old acquaintances. We are not searching for buried treasure or digging up old scandal."

"Your former acquaintances are apparently up to their old tricks, if your characterization of camp life is any indication. Petty dramas of every description, I believe you said."

"A tryst among the well born English is hardly a petty drama."

We reached the chilly grandeur of the foyer, in part because St. Sevier had traveled at a good clip from the scene on the steps.

"Millicent is Scottish, Patrick is Irish," I said.

"*Patrick.*"

"Mr. O'Dea. The lieutenant, surveyor, botanist, lover-at-large, and wheedler without portfolio *or* coat."

St. Sevier stopped at the top of the curving staircase. "O'Dea cut a swath with the ladies. Annie said it wasn't all charm and flirtation either."

"Honestly, St. Sevier, I know of no adult male who willingly limits himself to charm and flirtation where pretty women are concerned, unless he prefers men, and even then—"

St. Sevier put a finger to my lips. "We saw nothing, we heard nothing, and if we stand here arguing long enough, your English stubbornness and native curiosity will see that we have nothing to eat as well."

"I am determined and persistent," I said, allowing myself a little flounce down the steps. "Besides, my native curiosity, as you call it, has located two missing spouses and solved a vexatious spree of thefts at an otherwise dull house party. You have enjoyed—"

He stopped me at the bottom of the steps with a hand on my arm. "Violet, please do not look for a hornet's nest to poke with your parasol. I hoped a visit to Rutland Wood would appeal to you as a means of putting off your return to London, but I fear your dread of London is simply a dread of placid domesticity."

We had somehow progressed from bantering to a genuine disagreement. "What do you mean?"

"I make an observation." He had also made himself into the

embodiment of Gallic dignity. "You enjoy the intrigues you stir up, no matter that they can be dangerous."

"I don't stir up anything. I don't kidnap brides, impersonate errant grooms, steal baubles out of a need for attention... You are not being fair, St. Sevier."

Nor was he being honest. Something about that tryst we'd interrupted had turned St. Sevier protective and cautious. His past doubtless informed the scene in a way I could not fathom.

"I am not wrong," he said, trying for a smile. "A woman who was once afraid to leave her own home would now be happy to turn a rural palace upside down. We are guests passing through here, Violet, while our hosts are the center of a household and a community we are not part of. Please do not borrow trouble, or purchase it by the yard wholesale, as you are wont to do."

St. Sevier lectured me about borrowing trouble, while Patrick O'Dea had apparently borrowed Thomas MacNeil's *wife*, and the lady had similarly borrowed Kathleen O'Dea's husband.

"I promise you this," I said, starting off across the foyer, "I am in no mood to untangle anybody's troubles. I am in the mood to demolish a plate of eggs and have you to myself for the morning. Perhaps tomorrow we can hack out together, though I'm also to be subjected to the edifying experience of a tour of the grounds with Mrs. O'Dea. If you could join that exciting adventure, I'd appreciate it."

St. Sevier—damn his long legs—kept pace with me easily. "You have taken offense at a reasonable request on my part. I suppose I now must jolly you back into an agreeable humor?"

"Now you must trust me to exercise the common sense God gave a goat, much less the discretion any earl's daughter learns before she leaves the schoolroom. Why must this house be so perishing enormous?"

"You are easily vexed when hungry. Your delicate feminine humors become unbalanced."

"While you wax medically pompous with no provocation whatsoever. I will arm-wrestle you for the toast rack." The scent of bacon wafted up the corridor, and I was tempted to break into an unladylike trot.

"I would win," St. Sevier said, "and feed you the toast from my hand as you sat purring in my lap."

"Just for that, I will spill tea on your lap at some moment when you least expect it." Even as I enjoyed our return to pleasant bickering, I realized that St. Sevier was distracting me from the scene on the landing and the questions it had raised.

Did Kathleen O'Dea or Thomas MacNeil *know* their spouses were intimately cavorting, and if so, did anybody care? I had never reconciled myself to my husband's multiple, simultaneous infidelities, but I was not a former army wife, inured to hardship and a dislocation of social norms.

What was Patrick O'Dea's *bright idea*?

Was Millicent MacNeil a reluctant lover, manipulating Patrick for her own ends, or something else? I could not forget the ambiguity of her posture—half flirtation, half weary resignation.

My musings were abruptly set aside upon gaining the breakfast parlor. The only occupants were Thomas MacNeil and Kathleen O'Dea, and both were smiling as MacNeil poured the lady a cup of tea. I marshaled my most gracious store of dignified conviviality and smiled right back at them.

St. Sevier held my chair, buttered his toast, and embarked on a polite rapture regarding the weather, resorting to French every fifth or sixth word.

CHAPTER FOUR

"The views are magnificent," Lady Rutland said, topping up Mr. Jones's teacup, "though they are mostly views of sheep, hillsides, and sky. You'll want a proper cloak if you're planning on climbing to the lookout, though. The heights are windy, and we cannot have you taking a chill."

"At least we've a doctor in residence if that should happen," Daphne Jones remarked. She was the smallest of the four women I had met at the Wood, but she made up in energy what she lacked in stature. The melodious timbre of her Welsh accent was belied by an efficiency of movement—she chewed her ham with dispatch, she stirred her coffee briskly.

Of all the ladies at the Wood, Daphne Jones was the one St. Sevier had singled out for praise.

"In my experience," St. Sevier said, "one is more likely to fall ill from a lack of exercise than from regular doses of fresh air."

"I'll fetch my cloak," I said, "and take some of that fresh air on the terrace."

Millicent rose as well. "I'm for the wage books. Tomorrow is wage day for the ladies, and one must be prepared."

I did not want to be alone with Millicent, who had sauntered into the breakfast parlor on her own and greeted Patrick O'Dea with cheerful indifference not a quarter hour later. O'Dea had by then shaved and donned neckcloth and coat, and his greeting to the company was also one of amiable ease.

"I hate wage day," Millicent muttered as we traversed the corridor. "Thomas is a quartermaster by trade and inclination, and the click of the abacus is music to his soul. He handles the men's wages and the senior staff's wages, while I have been delegated the *exercise* of paying the female domestics."

"You prefer not to handle money?" Ladies didn't, and being married to a man who did not precisely work with his hands, Millicent was a lady in name.

She sent me a sidewise look. "We Scots learn not to turn up our noses at hard-earned coin. I simply don't care to spend my entire morning passing out packets. I have it down to a system, so the employee tells me her station, and I pass over an appropriate packet. I will spend today counting out the wage for an underchambermaid a dozen times over. Twice that number of packets for the chambermaids proper, half a dozen for the scullery maids.

"The Wood employs legions of female domestics," she went on, "and every one of them must bob a curtsey at me when she collects her pay. By the end of the morning, my neck aches from nodding in return. Perhaps I should apply to the doctor for a remedy."

Had I not seen Millicent on the stair with O'Dea, the remark would have been harmless. Because she nudged my arm and grinned, and because I *had* seen her *in flagrante delicto*, I did not care for her innuendo.

"St. Sevier will probably tell you to apply some horse liniment."

"But he'd do so gallantly, and he would carefully examine the ailing part first. We all love St. Sevier, you know. Athena fell for him hard. Alas, he is French, and an English general's daughter cannot marry a Frenchman, not even a handsome émigré devoted to the British cause."

Millicent remained lodged at my side as I ascended the main staircase. It occurred to me she was waiting for me to mention having caught her in O'Dea's embrace, an admission I wasn't about to make. No poking my parasol at hornets' nests—doctor's orders.

I paused at the top of the steps, dearly hoping Millicent's path and mine were about to part. "I doubt St. Sevier was as devoted to the British cause or to the French cause so much as he was devoted to saving lives and alleviating suffering."

"He did a lot of both," Millicent said. "Disease killed as many men as the battlefield generally, but not in our regiments. St. Sevier would not be shouted down by the sergeants who grumbled about having to trudge a quarter mile downstream to heed nature's call. The laundresses were not to do washing upstream from camp, and oh, he had a whole list of proscriptions and orders. Even stuck his nose into decisions such as where to graze the horses. He caused some talk in the officers' mess."

"But Lord Rutland listened to him, and lives were saved."

Millicent gazed down into the empty foyer, a white marble space full of light and expensive art, all to impress visitors with the Wood's patently obvious grandeur.

"Lives saved for what purpose?" she asked. "To charge headlong into enemy fire. I wasn't as conscientious about visiting the infirmary as Daphne was, but I took my shifts. St. Sevier once told me that his purpose in serving medically was to gather up some small influence to use if any of his brothers were captured. You should ask him about that."

The next two weeks began to loom not as a pleasant respite in beautiful surrounds, but as a forced march on short rations.

"St. Sevier does not care to dwell much on his army days," I replied, "and I have a cloak to fetch."

I had turned to go when Millicent's voice stopped me. "Does Hugh still have nightmares? Thomas does, though not as often."

The question was a trap, or two traps. I was to ask how Millicent knew that *Hugh* had ever had nightmares—something few but a lover would learn of—and I was to reveal whether I was in a position to relay the present state of his affliction.

"You'll have to ask him," I said, starting off down the corridor. "Ancient history is not a topic that comes up between us very often."

Millicent saluted me with an odd smile and went the other direction, thank the merciful powers.

The woman had a handsome, good-natured Scottish husband and had apparently earned the regard of a smiling, devilishly attractive Irishman as well. Why must she pry around the edges of my relationship with St. Sevier and remind me that I could never fully understand his past?

But then, I had been married to a handsome, genial man, and I had been miserable as his wife. Perhaps I ought not to judge Millicent too harshly.

I traded my shawl for a light cloak of brown merino wool and used the maids' stairs to make my way to the back terrace. Despite St. Sevier admonishing me to mind my own business, I was struck by the folly of any couple disporting where the staff could come upon them.

First thing in the day, maids were all a-bustle, bringing trays up to bedrooms, toting buckets of coal to hearths almost extinguished, carrying the previous day's clothing to the laundry, and so forth. To tarry with a lover on the stairs at such an hour had been foolish or daring, particularly with other guests also biding at the Wood.

I found a bench on the wide back terrace and jettisoned such thoughts from my mind, focusing instead on the orderly beds of colorful tulips. A half-dozen gardeners were at work trimming hedges, watering potted heartsease, weeding beds, and otherwise tending to the splendor before me.

A mason parged a pattern of vines and leaves over the base of the central fountain, and another man oiled the hinges of the tall wrought-iron gates at the distant back of the main walk.

So much activity and expense. The manor I'd visited in Scotland had had a walled garden one-quarter this size and three times more pleasing. Derwent Hall's garden was more modest yet, and all the more inviting for being of a manageable dimension.

"Did you refrain from brawling with Mrs. MacNeil?" St. Sevier asked, ambling out onto the terrace.

"Barely. She asked if you still have nightmares."

He offered me a hand, and I took it to rise from the bench, though I'd been standing and sitting unassisted since the age of two. His courtesy was for show, in case anybody was gawking out of windows, and for me, in case I was preparing to launch into a tirade.

"We all have nightmares, Violet." He tucked my hand over his arm and led me down the steps. "I frequently slept in the infirmary. Everybody heard my troubled dreams. Think nothing of it."

"You were not her lover?"

St. Sevier seemed amused. "I have already told you I was not. Nor the lover of any of the ladies or the gentlemen. And yes, that went on in the king's army, mostly because nobody wanted to have to march while suffering a bad case of the bachelor's pox."

"I am beginning to think Napoleon was the least of the military's woes."

"You would not be entirely wrong."

We strolled along, the gravel crunching beneath our boots, until we came to the back gates. The man tending to the hinges was still up on his ladder, though he took off his cap as we approached.

"Be that our own Doc Frenchie! Damned if 'tisn't! Sir, a pleasure to see you." He bustled down from his perch and approached, hand outstretched. "I'd heard there was company from the old days, a medical man, but to see you again, sir. 'Tis a fine, fine day indeed."

St. Sevier shook and also touched the man on the arm. "Sergeant Bevins, you look well."

The fellow actually looked a bit piratical. He had a patch over one eye, and his hair was tied back in an old-fashioned queue. He was not old, but rather, weathered into an indefinable age. Some gray showed at his temples, while his smile revealed perfect teeth. His build was the stolid, modest stature of a yeoman and his clothing equally serviceable.

"I can still see out of both eyes," he said, flipping up his patch. "I wear the patch in bright light, like you told me, and it hardly pains me at all as long as I don't read too much Holy Scripture. My arm works nearly as good as new too." Bevins's smile turned fierce. "Doc Frenchie wouldn't let them saw it off, he saved my eye. The bastards wanted that, too, pardon my language, missus."

He readjusted his patch and beamed at St. Sevier. "Peacetime agrees with you, Doc, or perhaps some time in parson's mousetrap has put the meat on your bones."

"I am remiss," St. Sevier said. "Lady Violet Belmaine, may I make known to you Sergeant Thaddeus Bevins. Bevins, her ladyship is visiting the Wood with me."

Bevins recollected his manners enough to bob in my direction. "Take good care of our doc, milady. He took good care of us. Didn't care if a fellow was enlisted or some nabob's commissioned sprat. Doc done right by us all."

I appreciated honesty, and anybody who cared for St. Sevier need not stand on ceremony with me. "I will take the very best care of Monsieur that I can, Sergeant."

"Does Rutland take care of his people here?" St. Sevier asked. "I've seen at least three familiar faces among the house staff."

Bevins shrugged. "We aren't at war, but some things don't change. Mutton, tatties, and applesauce in the mess hall. Bickering in the ranks and either too much to do or not enough. We manage."

That was hardly a glowing endorsement. "Surely the diet offers more variety than that?" I asked. Bevins peered past my shoulder at gardens awash in imported flowers. "Our produce goes to the hotels and hostelries once the hillwalkers arrive. Autumn fare is decent at the Wood. I've eaten worse and been grateful. Best get back to work, or the colonel will be having a word with me."

He slapped his cap on his head and moved the ladder to the opposite side of the gate.

We had been dismissed.

St. Sevier, perhaps knowing I wanted to question Bevins further —nobody employed by a thriving estate was expected to work all day on mutton, potatoes, and applesauce, supper after supper, were they? —took me by the hand and led me down the path.

Spruce Manor fit its name, in so far as the property was in every bit as good trim as was Rutland Wood. While the Wood was a palace, Spruce Manor was a Tudor retreat. The mullioned windows sparkled, the pots of heartsease were placed at precise intervals along the circular drive, every snow-white curtain was tied back at the same angle.

The Manor lay in a hollow between two sheep-dotted swales of spring grass. No forest encroached on its sunny serenity, though its park shared frontage on the same lake that bordered part of the Wood. I knew this because St. Sevier and I had made the climb to the lookout that morning, and the pattern of the Wood's surrounds had revealed itself.

Beyond the oasis formed by the Wood, its outbuildings, and the neighboring Spruce Manor, this corner of the district belonged to sheep, small lakes or meres, and more sheep. Where the forest had been scraped or grazed away, the grassy hillsides were bare to the sky, and the general impression was one of bleakness.

"The hillwalkers have started to arrive," Daphne Jones said, sipping her tea. "We love them, and we wish them a safe journey back to the south. More tea?"

I accepted a second cup. She had served a delicate China black, fresh shortbread, and sandwiches without crusts, just as any Mayfair hostess might have. Her drawing room was similarly appointed with cutwork, framed dried flowers, and a portrait of some uniformed old fellow over the mantel, a bewigged, powdered, and panniered lady at his side.

Daphne Jones's parlor was further distinguished by a pair of sizable cats. One of them, a splendid marmalade specimen, lounged on the mantel, while the other—all black with green eyes—perched sphinxlike on a hassock.

I enjoyed cats. They were consistently and shamelessly self-interested, nothing of deceit about them. They were also generally quiet, handsome, and soft to the touch, as well as lethal when on the hunt. A cat would accept hospitality from a human, or go catch its own supper on a whim, as if to remind one and all that a feline was ever to be treated as an honored guest.

Daphne Jones apparently liked cats, too, for when the marmalade fellow leaped down from the mantel, his next choice of perch was her lap.

"Daphne denies her favorites nothing," Lady Rutland said. "She puts me in mind of my father, who was quite the disciplinarian, except with his own ladies. My sisters and I were spoiled without limit."

Daphne stroked the cat, who'd begun a prodigious rumbling. "How can growing girls be spoiled in military camps and forts?"

"Canada wasn't like Spain," Lady Rutland said. "No great battles, no scorching heat. The winters were interminable, but we learned to cope with that. One conquered entire sonatas in the course of a Canadian winter. The intricacies of the quadrille were a relief from boredom, though I must say the northern lights were amazing. Might I have a spot more tea as well?"

The cat sent me a look, one that suggested fond reminiscing was as much a part of the tea ritual in these surrounds as the shortbread and sandwiches.

Daphne topped up Lady Rutland's cup, despite the beast draped across mine hostess's lap. "St. Sevier looks to be in quite good spirits," she remarked, putting the pot back on the tray. "He has gained at least two stone, and it looks wonderful on him."

What was I to say to that, for both ladies were looking to me for a reply, as was the cat. "From what St. Sevier has told me, army life presented as many challenges as it did rewards."

"You know he was married?" Daphne asked.

"His past is not my affair, but yes, I know he was married, and his Annie was killed in a skirmish with a French patrol."

"You will forgive us if we're protective of him," Lady Rutland said. "That man saved lives regardless of which uniform a soldier wore, argued generals into producing medical supplies at great cost, and never asked anything for himself. He and Annie were not a love match, not by any means, but her death took something out of him that all the battles and diseases could not."

I was supposed to ask what *not a love match, not by any means* signified, and I would ask. I would ask St. Sevier, if and when the moment was right.

"Marriage can deal intimate wounds of a kind not easily treated," I said. "St. Sevier has apparently made his peace with the past."

The ladies exchanged an unreadable look, much like a pair of cats might.

"They fought," Mrs. Jones went on, as if I hadn't spoken. "Annie wanted him to take her back to Scotland. He was unwilling to desert troops sorely, sorely in need of competent medical support. I don't think he minded so much that she left him, but he blamed himself for her death."

"Soldiers drink," Lady Rutland added. "They drink for courage and to forget and because they can. Not St. Sevier. He *worked*. If there was no work at the surgery, he called on the new mothers—there are always new mothers in a camp of any size—or foraged for medicinal herbs. He found the local physicians or herbwomen and spoke to them of their practices and lore. He was a man driven."

Daphne lifted the cream pitcher from the tray and poured a few teaspoons of cream onto the polished oak floor. Her feline friend rose, stretched luxuriously, and deigned to hop down and lick up the offering.

"To be a healer at war," Daphne said, watching her cat lap at the cream, "is a recipe for madness. Annie's dramatics did not help."

"She was young," Lady Rutland murmured, sipping her tea. "Young people can be stubborn."

"Stupid," Daphne countered. "What woman, having lost one husband on the battlefield, then thinks it a fine idea to travel overland without a proper escort in the midst of two warring armies, winter coming on, and rations in short supply. She's lucky her fate was a bullet."

Lady Rutland set down her teacup. "We don't know what her fate was. If she was lucky, she expired quickly from a well-placed bullet or bayonet."

The cat finished his cream and leaped into my lap, which was a mercy. The beast gave me something to do with my hands, someplace to look, while I reeled with an impulse to tell these pretty, friendly women to shut their damned mouths.

Hugh's wife had not merely been killed in a pointless skirmish—if such a death could ever be considered *mere*—she had likely been violated, possibly repeatedly, before expiring.

"Ladies," I said, gathering the cat into my arms, "it is not your place to tell me these things. If St. Sevier cares to share past tragedies with me, that is his business, and you do him no favors with these disclosures."

Lady Rutland's brows rose, while Daphne Jones smiled faintly.

"I can tell by the way he watches you," Daphne said, "that he is smitten, but where Hugh St. Sevier is concerned, it would not do for only one party to be smitten."

"Forgive us," Lady Rutland said. "Old habits die hard, and in the army, we might bicker and brawl amongst ourselves, but we close ranks against all foes when one of our own has been threatened."

"How very presuming of you both," I retorted as the cat rubbed his head against my chin, "to decide that I am a foe and that St.

Sevier, a man of the world and wealthy in both wisdom and means, could not make that determination for himself."

"Gracious." Daphne's smile faded. "I believe that qualifies as a drumhead court-martial, Athena. My lady, I apologize for our blunt speech. We would hate to see St. Sevier brought low again by misplaced affection."

"The apology you owe is to him," I said. "You discuss personal aspects of his past with a woman you do not know, and you do so without asking his permission. Not well done of you."

Lady Rutland was for once not looking so serene. "We are sorry, but when Annie left, St. Sevier went quietly to pieces. We went to pieces not knowing what to do for him. It was a bad time."

Wellington's army had taken years to push its way from Portugal across Spain into France. That these ladies would recall the end of St. Sevier's marriage as *a bad time* suggested their motives were genuine and that my darling Hugh had suffered considerably indeed.

"I do not question your devotion to an old friend," I said, "but rather, your means of looking after him. Ask him how he goes on, ask him why he's willing to accompany a rather dull widow on a prosaic journey. He will answer you honestly."

"No," Lady Rutland said, "he won't. He will turn up all gentlemanly discretion, fob us off with flirtation, and go about his business however he pleases to. He is but a man."

That was not fair to Hugh, who—unlike my father, brothers, or late husband—did not fob me off with flirtation. He instead told me plainly when he wasn't feeling like very good company, and I was honored that it was so.

"Speak to me of life in the Lake District," I said, setting the cat on the floor. "I hear of hillwalkers. I see a prodigious quantity of sheep. Against what real foes does one campaign here, and how do you occupy yourselves of a winter?"

I was changing the subject, usurping the place of my hostesses rather than belabor their errors where St. Sevier was concerned. I was angry with them for meddling, and I hurt for Hugh, who had suffered at war even more than I'd known. I was also aware that I had the balance of a two-week visit to endure and thus was unwilling to be any more disagreeable than I had already been.

I wanted the call to be over, the day to be over, the visit to be over, and yet, I was still not eager to return to London.

CHAPTER FIVE

"These people are protective of you," I said as Hugh fell in step beside me on the path from the stable to the house. "The ladies made very certain I knew the particulars of your matrimonial past. I am not to toy with you, or I shall be drummed out of the corps." Or something.

"I like it when you toy with me. I like better when we toy with each other behind a locked door, shutting out the world and all its follies."

"The fresh air is making you frisky." While I was restless, despite an active day. St. Sevier had gone rowing with Rutland and seemed relaxed and happy as a result of his exertions. "Did you mention to Rutland that scene on the stairs this morning?"

"Why would I do that?"

"Because it's dissension in the ranks? His surveyor or botanist, or whatever O'Dea calls himself, is cavorting with the steward's wife. This cannot be good for morale."

"You are bothered by what you saw?" St. Sevier led me to a bench that faced the glass wall of the conservatory, not an exactly pleasing prospect. The larger potted plants—citrus trees, a few squat pineapples, some enormous ferns—were mashed up against the glass like fish struggling to find space in an aquarium. A row of half barrels of red and blue salvia sitting along the terrace outside the wall did nothing to ameliorate the sense of desperation and disorder within.

"I was bothered by what I saw," I said, thinking back over the day. "I was more bothered by the great good cheer at the breakfast table afterward. We see O'Dea all but enjoying himself with Millicent MacNeil in a stairwell, then it's 'pass the butter' and 'what lovely weather' fifteen minutes later with their spouses at breakfast."

St. Sevier ranged an arm along the back of the bench. "Does this have to do with Belmaine?"

"Spare me from perceptive Frenchmen." Freddie had frequently come to breakfast having just washed off the perfume from his previous evening's disporting.

"Rutland would not intervene, *mon coeur.* Enlisted men could be disciplined without mercy, but squabbles among officers were often ignored, and nobody is squabbling."

"To the contrary, all seems pleasant domestic accord. When Mr. Jones joined us for a stroll in Spruce Manor's gardens, he bowed over my hand, but he kissed both his wife and Lady Rutland on the cheek."

"Were you jealous?" This was becoming a theme with St. Sevier, suggesting exactly what he and his Ann had argued about so incessantly.

"Hardly. I know rural manners among close friends are informal, but please do not think I want your old acquaintances kissing my cheek without invitation."

"Violet, my old friends are not fools. No man would presume with you to that extent and live to tell of his folly. I found myself absorbed in a different sort of puzzle from the intrigues at Rutland Wood."

Puzzle? St. Sevier had used the word knowingly, like those drops of cream left on the floor for Daphne Jones's cat.

"You wonder how they entertain themselves of a winter hereabouts?" I suggested. I knew how Patrick O'Dea and Millicent MacNeil likely entertained themselves.

"How do they afford all this splendor?" St. Sevier replied. "Rutland employs an army, he provides a gentleman's livelihood for at least three of his former direct reports, and the standards here are quite comfortable. All I see to support this luxury is a lot of sheep. The price of wool has plummeted now that the army isn't outfitting one-tenth of the male populace in uniforms."

"One-sixth, if you count the local militias." Britain had somehow found the funds for those uniforms and could keep half-pay officers employed by the thousands, but maimed veterans from the enlisted ranks went begging in the streets of London.

"Peacetime has not been good for the wool industry," St. Sevier said, crossing his legs at the ankle. "Added to that, over the past few decades, most of the world has developed sheep breeds well suited to the native climate, and you have a collapsed British wool market."

"And yet, Rutland's conservatory remains full of exotic fruits, his gardens are awash in color, and paying his inside female domestics alone takes half the day. Lady Rutland is an heiress, though, is she not?"

"General Grossnickel is still quite hale, and even coal prices aren't what they once were."

Perhaps the family wasn't waiting for the general to rest in the arms of his fathers before disseminating some of his wealth. Then too, Lady Rutland would have brought substantial settlements to her marriage, some of which would have been available to Rutland immediately following the nuptials.

"Are you truly curious regarding the estate finances," I asked, "or simply trying to distract me from Patrick O'Dea's philandering?"

"Millicent MacNeil was doing a bit of philandering too, my lady."

I did not share St. Sevier's impression of Mrs. MacNeil's attitude, but then, O'Dea had been intent on wheedling some concession from her. I had yet to meet the woman who truly enjoys a wheedling male, much less one undertaking his campaign while half dressed.

"Bevins's comment," St. Sevier said, "about mutton and potatoes stuck with me. Mutton and potatoes make sense, but no turnips? No bread and butter? No cinnamon rolls on Sunday? Rutland didn't spoil his men, but he knew marching on an empty belly made for poor fighting spirit. He also heard more than one lecture from me about the need for fresh fruits and vegetables to ward off scurvy."

I thought back to the conversation over tea, to women concerned for a man with a healing vocation who'd lost his wife and nearly lost his sanity too in the midst of war.

"I don't care if the wool market has collapsed," I said, taking St. Sevier's hand. "If that is the price of peace, I will accept it, and I hope the rest of Britain feels the same way." Easy for me to say, given the wealth associated with my station, but markets rose and collapsed all the time. Something as lowly as tulips had occasioned economic upheaval, and of course the world would learn to raise its own sheep and corn.

St. Sevier had adjusted to his losses. Britain could adjust to a peacetime economy.

"Did you enjoy your call at Spruce Manor?" St. Sevier asked, kissing my knuckles.

"Not particularly. The ladies once again had to impress upon me that I am not military, and they knew you when you were young and dashing."

"You wound me."

"You have graduated from dashing to debonair, and thank heavens you are not so painfully young, else I would be too ancient to merit your notice." I was soon to turn six and twenty, and thus my provenance had originated in biblical times.

"I will take your ancient self out on the lake tomorrow," St. Sevier said, rising and offering me his hand. "Talk of scurvy has put me in mind of oranges. Will you steal one with me?"

The season was late for oranges, but a wander in the conservatory suited me. Oranges were quite delectable, and I had a mind to steal a kiss or two and to hug St. Sevier tightly where nobody could see us. We entered the conservatory by a side door, and I immediately indulged my impulse.

St. Sevier hugged me back gently. "What is this about?"

"You are so dear. So very, very dear to me." And he had served honorably, as a *volunteer*, pursuing his profession where it was most needed and impressing one and all with his skill and dedication.

"I must take you traveling to the Lakes more often if the result is to unleash your affectionate nature."

I kissed him to stop his trivializing, and simply because kissing St. Sevier was a fine idea on its own merits. "I don't have an affectionate nature. My husband lamented that lack many times, but I have high regard for you, Hugh St. Sevier."

"Your husband was... *C'était un idiot*. Let's find an orange, shall we?" He kept hold of my hand, and we struck off down a paving-stone path. We were approaching the little parlor arrangement at the center of the conservatory when St. Sevier came to a halt and put a finger to his lips.

I peeked around him and saw Lord Rutland entwined with Kathleen O'Dea on the chaise, his lordship gently caressing Mrs. O'Dea's breast. Mrs. O'Dea's palm was enjoying a similarly close acquaintance with his lordship's falls, or with the male tumescence disarranging them. They made a languid, tender, and shocking tableau.

I backed away, tugging St. Sevier with me, and managed not to speak until we were outside the building.

"Perhaps they endure their northern winters by holding orgies," I said, stalking toward the house. "St. Sevier, what manner of people are your friends that we come upon not one but two illicit trysts in the course of a day?"

St. Sevier was silent until we reached the back terrace, where-upon he slanted a puzzled glance in the direction of the conservatory.

"O'Dea had a reputation as a charmer, but that Rutland would disport with... Perhaps Kathleen is seeking revenge for Patrick's wandering?"

"Oh, of course. Blame the woman. What Kathleen sought—and Rutland obligingly offered—was a tumble in the conservatory. I grow reluctant to drink the tea in this house, for fear it contains an aphrodisiac."

St. Sevier leaned close enough to whisper in my ear. "Drink the tea, *mon ange*. We shall contrive as best we can to deal constructively with any side effects."

"Moaning and wailing belowstairs," Lucy said, drawing my walking dress over my head. "Such tears as you never heard, my lady, but then, when two dozen chambermaids get to sniffling and howling, the racket is deafening." She laid my wrinkled walking dress on the bed and passed me a dressing gown.

"Why the drama?" I asked, belting the robe around my middle.

"Three of 'em was let go this morning. Given their packet with a bit extra, free room and board until the wagons make the trip down to Lancaster next week for provisions, and stage fare anywhere in Britain. More than most employers would do."

Three at once? Even if the Wood had three dozen chambermaids, sacking three at once would mean more work for those remaining. "Were they let go for poor performance?"

I hated discharging an employee, but had learned to do so with those who habitually slacked, overimbibed, or made themselves disagreeable to the rest of the staff. One footman intent on bothering a scullery maid was one too many.

"They were all given glowing characters signed by Lady Rutland herself, but the maids are very much vexed over it."

I would be vexed to be turned out into the world on short notice with only a few coins and a means of returning to my father's house, my figurative tail between my legs.

"What are you in the mood for tonight, my lady?" Lucy asked, opening the wardrobe doors. "The blue is becoming and the gray quite elegant."

In Scotland, I hadn't bothered much over my attire. The household I'd visited, for all its troubles, had been friendly and informal. On formal occasions, the menfolk had sported kilts, the ladies tartan finery. That sort of uniform precluded the jockeying for notice that Mayfair modistes made their living on.

"The raspberry," I said. "It is both elegant and eye-catching." Also a bit daring, but I was in the mood to remind my hostess that she entertained an earl's daughter, not a young and unhappy army wife prone to histrionics.

"With the ruby drop necklace and earbobs," Lucy said, withdrawing a lush velvet creation from the wardrobe and laying it over the chaise. "One of my favorites, and past time you wore it again. Don't bother demanding a fichu."

"Right," I said, opening my dressing gown to untie the petticoat I'd worn throughout the day. "A shawl only, which I remove at dinner, like a cover removed from the fish course to start the meal."

"More like a dessert course," Lucy rejoined. "Let me unlace you."

She managed that job with a dispatch St. Sevier never displayed, thank heavens, and sent me behind the privacy screen to wash and to change into the lacy chemise that provided the foundation for my evening wardrobe.

I tarried with my soap and water and applied a light perfume redolent of cedar. The scent reminded me of my time in Scotland, and in particular of Sebastian MacHeath, Marquess of Dunkeld. As much as I treasured the days and nights spent with St. Sevier, I had hated parting from Sebastian.

The marquess had a tolerant, pragmatic outlook on life and an irreverent sense of humor. He would be amused at the goings-on here at the Wood and contribute his share to the storytelling.

I emerged from the privacy screen and submitted to the ordeal of being relaced, this time in a corset finished in satin, the better to allow fabric to slide over fabric when I moved.

"This corset is not my favorite." Freddie had had it made for me, probably by the same modistes who'd clothed his several mistresses. The satin was not quite red, more mulberry, which hardly made it less scandalous.

"These stays flatter you," Lucy retorted. "Shows what deserves showing off." She passed me a petticoat for evening wear, all lacy hems and soft underflounce. "A woman has to manage as best she can, lest she be turned off without notice, so to speak."

St. Sevier was courting me with a view toward marriage, not information Lucy was privy to. If and when he changed his mind about that objective, he would not turn me off without a character.

"Lucy, you will refrain from commenting on private matters." A wish more than an order, of course.

"What private matters? The Wood has apparently been letting maids go regular-like for the past half year, but no footmen. *Economies*, according to the lady's maids. If you ask me, sacking a footman saves more money than sacking a parlor maid."

I stepped into the petticoat, and Lucy set about tying it off to the side. Lucy had a valid point. "Sacking an underbutler would likely save even more," I said.

"Lady Rutland's maid, Walters, explained it to me. Firstly, there are few jobs a maid can do that a footman cannot, such as hauling coal or emptying chamber pots. Footmen can beat rugs, make beds, blacken andirons... Anything a maid can do, a footman can do as well, though he might grumble about doing women's work."

"He would not merely grumble," I said. "He would set up a lament heard in the celestial realm itself, do a poor job, and then ask some female—a maid, an underhousekeeper—to explain the task to him. She would finish up his job while also tending to her own. I've seen it done."

"That's as may be, but maids cannot do all the chores the footmen do—climbing on ladders to clean the outside windows or scrub the molding in the library, carrying the heaviest trays, moving furniture about, or carrying the rugs outside to be beaten."

Actually, maids could and did do all those things. "Many a household runs quite well without a footman to its name."

"Not many a grand household, besides—hold still—Walters says that's not the whole of it." Lucy eased the dress over my head and stepped around back to start on the hooks. "Many of the male staff took the king's shilling, and some even served under Lord Rutland himself. Letting the fellows go won't do, so it's the maids given the sack."

Given the sack, like extraneous wives and laundresses left behind in France when the military no longer had a use for them.

"If the objective is economies," I said, "then pruning the senior ranks makes more sense than sacking underlings." The dress fit me superbly, a result of the contour of the boning in Freddie's infernal corset. He had known his way around the female body, had Freddie.

"Right," Lucy said, tucking this and hooking that. "But sacking senior staff is nearly scandalous out here in the shires. Walters said letting the maids go now means they can find seasonal work at the hotels catering to the hillwalkers. Gives the maid time to write to family and notify the agencies if she doesn't want to leave the area. An underbutler or lady's maid won't find a new post hereabouts half so easily."

"Somebody has given this business of sacking maids a great deal of thought." Or troubled to publicize their justifications for it.

"A dozen maids have been let go in the past six months, and two footmen left without being replaced. That is a lot of economies even at a place this size."

I thought back to St. Sevier's discourse on the collapsing wool market as Lucy did my hair in a half-up, half-down coiffure that required more patience from me and more pins than its appearance suggested.

"Why are we turning me out in such style tonight, Lucy?"

Because we were. This was the finest display I'd allowed since donning mourning more than two years past.

"Because it's time," Lucy said, affixing the ruby drop necklace so the jewel nestled at the top of my cleavage. She considered the look in the folding mirror, then let the ruby ease just a bit lower before doing up the clasp. "Because if half the talk belowstairs is to be believed, you are in the company of gentlemen who appreciate when a lady troubles over her appearance. Military men pay attention to turnout, you know."

"From what I've observed, some of them are so busy trying to get under a lady's skirts they don't trouble much to notice exactly what she's wearing."

Lucy fluffed the curls lying over my shoulder so they brushed the top of my breast. "You've heard the talk of Mr. Jones and Lady Rutland? He's apparently a great favorite with her, though from what I've seen, the lot of them are all quite chummy."

Athena and Mr. Jones? The same Garth Jones who'd presumed to kiss her ladyship's cheek earlier that day while his own wife looked on in bemused indifference?

Did that leave anybody without a trysting partner? I mentally sorted and tallied husbands and wives as I accepted a shawl of lavender silk from Lucy and made my way toward the guest parlor by way of the corridor. At the top of the steps, I encountered Mr. MacNeil, who wore a Stuart tartan kilt complete with tasseled sporran about his waist, ghillie brogues on his feet, and the ceremonial *sgian dubh* sheathed at his knee.

"My lady, will you permit me to escort you?" His blue eyes twinkled as he offered me his arm.

I tucked my hand around his elbow gingerly, glad indeed for my shawl, which I kept wrapped about my shoulders for the duration of the meal. Mr. MacNeil had been paired at supper with Daphne Jones, and to my discreetly goggling eye, they also appeared *quite* chummy.

I pleaded fatigue to allow myself to escape from withdrawing along with the rest of the ladies following the meal. Lucy tucked me into my own bed, and though I had intended to make my way down the balcony to St. Sevier's room, sleep overcame me betimes. Rather than intrude on St. Sevier first thing in the day, I took myself unaccompanied to the breakfast parlor.

"The deserter returns to camp," Millicent MacNeil said, smiling at me over her teacup. "Do have a seat before the locusts join us. We wore you out last night. I apologize for that. St. Sevier assured us that you simply seek solitude from time to time, being not all that long out of mourning. Tea?"

"No, thank you," I said, taking a plate at the sideboard. "I am in the mood for chocolate today." St. Sevier had promised to take me out on the water, and a cup of hot chocolate appealed as a start to a day out of doors.

"None to be had, I'm afraid, but I can have the kitchen send some up."

Well, drat. "What of coffee?"

"Of that, there is plenty. Rutland prefers it. Tommie likes ale with his morning steak, but don't let on that I said that. He tries not to be too Scottish around the others. O'Dea likes strong black tea, and Jones is unpredictable."

That Millicent knew the breakfast-table preferences of other women's husbands struck me as odd. She might easily notice Lord Rutland's habits, but I wasn't certain how my own brothers had taken to washing down their morning repasts in recent years.

But then, Millicent *knew* Patrick O'Dea, in the biblical sense. Had she also sampled Garth Jones's wares? Taken a turn in the conservatory with his lordship?

I dished out a modest portion of eggs, found a seat across from Millicent, and helped myself to a cup of coffee. She set the toast rack beside my plate, and as I buttered two slices, I wished for St. Sevier's company. He was an adept conversationalist, and already, I had become accustomed to starting my morning with him.

"We are to make a day of it on the water," Millicent announced. "The five couples, complete with picnic baskets. St. Sevier allowed as how this outing was your idea, and the other gentlemen took it up enthusiastically. Lady Rutland cast the deciding vote when she reminded us that the staff will be spring cleaning some of the Wood's public rooms starting today. I will sport an entire crop of freckles before sunset, and somebody's boat will capsize, mark me on this, my lady. Do you care for jam?"

"I do, actually."

She passed over a plate with three jam pots on it, one each of plum, pear, and marmalade. No forest fruits—raspberry was my favorite—which struck me as odd.

"I'm glad St. Sevier has brought you to visit us," Millicent said. "We grow too serious here, too focused on our little routines in our little world. It's a beautiful world, and left to our own devices, we forget that."

I busied myself applying the jam to my toast rather than inquiring whether frolicking with Patrick O'Dea was a serious endeavor. Perhaps Millicent had lost her heart to him, in which case she was to be pitied. Perhaps Kathleen O'Dea saved all her affections for Patrick's employer, in which case O'Dea's situation was not to be envied either.

I had been miserable enough in my marriage to wish every couple as much happiness as possible.

I cast around for a topic other than the weather. "My maid mentioned that your duties included letting a few of the domestic staff go yesterday. That is a difficult task."

Millicent pushed her eggs around on her plate. "I hate it. I know the lot of them can quit at will, that they go into domestic service knowing few posts last all that long, but still... They cry, and what am I to say to them? Rutland won't hear of thinning the ranks of footmen or gardeners, and Tommie grows weary of arguing with his lordship. It's a loud, thankless task."

"Might Mr. MacNeil seek another post?"

"Tommie isn't a steward by trade, my lady. He's an experienced quartermaster who has learned the knack of managing this one property, mostly by following his lordship around and doing what needs to be done. If we left the Wood, I doubt Rutland would write us a character—sets a lot of store by loyalty, does the colonel—and then where would we be?"

This conversation painted Millicent as something other than a lusty wife stepping out on her husband for a trivial affair. I liked the more thoughtful woman far better than the flirt, even though a discussion of her circumstances wasn't exactly cheerful. She described her situation as subtly trapped, because no steward would find employment without a character.

"I take it O'Dea and Jones are in similar circumstances?"

Millicent stirred her tea at length, and I realized I was to be treated to a half confidence. Not quite the truth, but not the counterfeit good cheer she exhibited in company.

"Patrick has nothing in Ireland. His family stole him blind while he was in Spain, and he won't prosecute his own blood. We're his family now, and he's Tommie's eyes and ears among the outside staff and in the village. Everybody talks to Patrick, and if you enjoy the gardens, the grounds, or the walking paths, that's thanks to Patrick."

Nobody missed home like an Irishman missed home, in my experience, though the Scots came a close second. O'Dea's family situation must have become bitter indeed.

"And Mr. Jones?" For surely he, too, had a tale.

"He is Rutland's man of business. Garth's family scraped together what they could to support him while he appprenticed to a solicitor. When his older brothers enlisted, Garth borrowed from his employer to finance a cornet's commission, thinking to look after the family hotheads. The brothers did not survive the war."

"And Mr. Jones never thought to return to Wales?"

"Inheriting under those circumstances created complications within the extended family. Garth let out the manor in Wales to pay off the loan. His sisters write to him, though his mother refuses to."

"Difficult." Was Garth Jones's situation at the Wood complicated by a particular fondness between Tommie MacNeil and Daphne Jones? I would never have asked such a thing and was spared from having to change the subject again by the arrival of more of the company. Mr. MacNeil escorted Lady Rutland, while St. Sevier sauntered in on his own.

"Lady Violet, good morning." Hugh bowed over my hand. "Your mention of some time on the water has inspired mass maneuvers later today. We are not to be underfoot when the great cleaning begins. I hope you don't mind that we will form part of an armada?"

He had been the one to mention taking me out in a boat, and I was honestly disappointed to learn that our private excursion was now to involve the whole regiment, or navy—whatever.

"As long as we don't encounter any hostile forces while at sea," I said.

MacNeil seated Lady Rutland and kissed his wife's cheek before taking the place beside me.

"Lady Violet, you must promise to be my crew. The gents will organize a wee race, and you and I shall prevail over the poseurs and pretenders bobbing in our wake. We'll send the lot of them to the bottom of the vasty deep."

Millicent passed her husband the teapot. "The lake is but ten feet deep in the middle, Lady Violet. Tommie is blustering."

"I'm actually trying to flirt a bit, darling wife, though Lady Violet looks less than moved by my efforts. Never fear, the Scots are a persistent lot. St. Sevier, surrender yonder honeypot, or Lady Violet will make ye walk the plank."

MacNeil's good humor lightened the mood, though I wasn't exactly looking forward to sharing a punt with him. I took my time with my meal, hoping to enjoy St. Sevier's company on the trek down to the lakeside. Lady Rutland took a hand in assigning escorts, however, and it fell to me to accompany Lord Rutland, while St. Sevier was honored to walk with Daphne Jones.

The rest of the party toddled off across the Wood's park, while I halted before leaving the front terrace. "My lord, if you will wait a moment, I will fetch my parasol. The sun on the water will be fierce, and I'd rather not send a servant for what I should have brought along in the first place."

Rutland waved a hand and perched on the balustrade, making a handsome picture in the morning sun. "Take your time, Lady Violet. The lake isn't going anywhere. A husband grows accustomed to these small delays."

I retrieved the desired article in short order and was soon strolling at Rutland's side. The memory of him disporting with Mrs. O'Dea crowded into my imagination and made casting about for a conversational gambit challenging.

I gave up the effort and instead left it to mine host to start a discussion on a topic of interest to him. The day was pretty, spring was gaining momentum, and I was prepared to enjoy myself in congenial, if somewhat frisky, company.

"Is St. Sevier courting you?" Lord Rutland asked.

Oh, delightful. Another interrogation. "You must put that question to him, my lord."

"I did. He replied in French, and my command of the vernacular is rusty. I believe he said, 'One can but try.'"

"I am not that long out of mourning, sir. Remarriage doesn't hold much appeal."

His lordship opened a gate for me, and we crossed from park to sheep pasture. "Remarriage is the triumph of hope over experience, to quote Dr. Johnson—who did not remarry after his bereavement. If I were to die, I'd wish Athena the joy of a subsequent union. She deserves to be happy, and any man would be delighted to find himself married to her."

Said the man who was delighted to cavort in the conservatory with his botanist's wife, and yet, Rutland sounded sincere. Men were like this. Some men. Freddie had professed to genuinely esteem and desire me, even as he'd dressed to enjoy the company of one mistress at the opera while planning to spend the balance of the evening with another.

Rutland came to a halt beside me. "For God's sake, what the hell is he about?"

Fifty yards down the path, Daphne Jones was plastered to St. Sevier in a fierce embrace. St. Sevier stroked her back gently and made no move to draw away.

"We'll take the drive down to the lake," I said, turning his lordship by the arm. "I have no wish to intrude on such a scene."

"They are old friends, Lady Violet. You must not make too much of a passing embrace. I doubt either Mrs. Jones or St. Sevier has anything to apologize for."

Rutland's words were polite and meant to be reassuring, but his tone conveyed that he was as troubled by what we'd seen as I was.

CHAPTER SIX

"Coming here was a mistake," St. Sevier said at the end of a long day spent mostly out of doors. "I was ready to pitch the lot of them into the lake before luncheon."

"The men act like brothers," I replied, taking yet another pin from my hair.

"Let me do that." St. Sevier ambled away from the window, and something about his walk suggested he was already thinking of intimate ways to put the frustrations of the day behind us.

I had my share of frustrations to deal with as well. "I can tend to my own hair, St. Sevier."

"Touching you soothes me. I had forgotten how much posturing and ridiculousness military men are capable of."

MacNeil and O'Dea had nearly capsized each other's vessels during the *wee race* the men undertook after luncheon. Jones and Lord Rutland had started an argument about the best wine to serve with roast fowl. O'Dea had deposited himself on Lady Rutland's blanket while his lordship argued, and that started a cascade of errant gentlemen that ended with Mr. Jones on my blanket.

Mr. Jones had thus been my escort for a constitutional along the lakeshore, and while he was a quiet man and a pleasant conversation-alist, his attention had repeatedly strayed to his wife, who was marching along, accompanied by O'Dea.

"The posturing and ridiculousness are not limited to military men," I said as St. Sevier ran his fingers through my hair. "I suspect two of my brothers have fought duels, and my father's dramatic gifts rival Mr. Garrick's in his heyday."

"Men of feeling," St. Sevier muttered, referring to a maudlin novel from an earlier age. "How the Englishman gained a reputation for emotional reticence is a very great mystery. One might even call it a deception." He withdrew the last of the pins in my hair, unbraided the loops and plaits Lucy had so artfully created, and then—devious, dear man—massaged my scalp.

"Was Rutland much given to drama as a commanding officer?"

"He raised his voice at incompetent subordinates often enough, but he was no petty martinet. He wasn't one for having the enlisted men flogged on a whim, though, and he well knew that Parliament wanted an accounting for any casualties."

The British army, unlike its Continental counterparts, had not had the luxury of conscription. British infantry and cavalry were made up entirely of recruits and volunteers. Excessive casualties would have been bad for business, so to speak.

Hugh took up the brush, and I let him soothe me—soothe us both. "How about the ladies?" I asked. "Were they given to drama on campaign?"

"Most were hearty, good-natured souls inured to camp life. My Ann was loud from time to time, but then, she was seventeen, far from home, and much disappointed."

I crossed my arms and lowered my forehead to rest on them. "You can talk about her with me, you know. I am forever maundering on about Freddie this and my late husband that." Less so, though, as time passed.

And ye gods, *seventeen*. I had married at seventeen, full of fond hopes for a sparkling future with my doting husband. That a young woman would marry and follow the drum at the same age was a testament to courage, love, or foolishness. Perhaps all three.

The fire in the hearth snapped and popped, and by the candlelight reflected in the folding mirror, St. Sevier's expression became wistful.

"Ann was a widow," he said. "Her husband was a young artillery sergeant whose foot was smashed when a green horse took exception to drawing a cannon into battle. The wound became septic, and there was Ann, pretty, without means, and widowed in the middle of Spain with winter coming on."

"You married her out of duty?"

"I was young too, Violet, and she was attractive, not merely pretty. She was the opposite of the sickness and death I dealt with every day. Ann was bold, determined, demanding, and lively. To her credit, she tried to be a wife to me."

I'd tried to be a wife to Freddie for five years, and the thought of abandoning him had never crossed my mind. Though, why not? Fashionable couples lived apart frequently.

"You married your Ann out of pity, though. Most women would hate that."

St. Sevier set aside the brush and divided my hair into three thick skeins. "I am still not sure entirely why I married her, but a committee of officers' wives put the notion to me, and I could not fault their reasoning. Much about army life is predicated on practicalities. Ann was a dissenting preacher's daughter fallen upon hard times, as the English say, and the men were regarding her with less than respectful intentions."

The relevance of Lady Rutland's cautionary tale became apparent. "They were dicing for her."

"And she was prepared to go bravely to her fate, which amounted to marriage or prostitution. I offered her an alternative choice of spouse, to the displeasure of half the regiment. Though I am French and was not a fighting man, she condescended to wed me."

"Do you miss her?"

Hugh had the knack of braiding my hair just right for nighttime. Tightly enough to remain tidy in bed, loose enough to be comfortable. It took him the whole length of my plait to come up with an answer.

"I think of her. I wonder if I might have done something different so that our parting might have been amicable rather than a desperate flight on her part. She was willing enough about welcoming me to her bed—I did ask, more than once—but was that in earnest, or was she resigned to entertaining one man instead of any in the camp with coin? I did not know her all that well, and yet, I bedded her all the same."

"And she bedded you. In the eyes of the world, she was an adult. Had she refused you, asked for time to get acquainted, or demanded a white marriage, you would have acceded to her wishes."

Hugh tied off my plait with a lavender hair ribbon. "I would. In this, you are correct. I have no patience with men who force women. I did not offer her passage back to Scotland, though, for which... hindsight bedevils a grieving mind. Ann had run off from her family, left them on bad terms. I had the sense, her only home at that point was with the army. She would have had no escort to the coast in any case."

He looped his arms around my shoulders and hugged me, his nose buried against my neck. "Are you indisposed, darling Violet? You did not come to me last night."

I loved that he would raise this topic, and so delicately. No accusations, no pouting, no difficult mood to decipher.

"I took to my own bed simply to rest my eyes for a moment and woke up the next morning in a lonesome condition. I spent all day longing for your company, and I wasn't about to make the same mistake tonight."

"I considered joining you," St. Sevier said, straightening, "but thought perhaps you wanted privacy. That business with Patrick O'Dea and Mrs. MacNeil put you out of sorts."

"As did that business with Lord Rutland and Kathleen O'Dea,

but I am also bothered to know that the Wood is reducing its staff of maids." I explained what Lucy had told me, while St. Sevier finished undressing and made use of the privacy screen.

"Rutland needs to diversify," St. Sevier said. "He could transport garden produce down to Lancaster in a day and to Liverpool or Manchester in another day traveling overland. By sea, the journey would likely be even faster, and the goods would arrive in better condition. Instead, he grows camellias and pineapples."

Camellias and pineapples had value too—enormous value in the case of pineapples.

"Come to bed," I said, rising and taking St. Sevier by the hand. "I am not sorry we came here, St. Sevier, because I know you better for spending time with you around your old army friends. They treasure you."

The ladies in particular doted on him, kept an eye on him, and found excuses to take his arm or ask his opinion. The men clearly respected him too. They bickered and taunted each other, but with St. Sevier, their touch was lighter and more humorous.

Any fool with a gun could and did take a life, but St. Sevier's skill —saving lives and repairing the gun's damage—was the more precious resource.

"They do not treasure me," he said, peeling out of his dressing gown. "They view me as an oddity, which I am."

I hung my dressing gown over his on the pegs on the bedpost. "You are my treasure. You should resume the practice of medicine, St. Sevier. You worked diligently to learn your art, you perfected it in a hard school, and the world needs skilled healers."

He looped his arms around my shoulders, his embrace weary and dear. "In France, one can be both a gentleman and an effective physician. Here? Physicians are little better than fortune-tellers who never truly examine their patients, and surgeons are one step above the knacker in social standing."

"You want to be an accoucheur. They have the standing of a physician while actually being of some use."

He led me to the bed and turned back the covers. "I love babies. You need to know this about me. If we marry, I want to be the favorite uncle of all your nieces and nephews, and I am jealous of Dunkeld because he will be the godfather of your nephew."

While I would be the boy's godmother. "Babies are a very great complication." I had had two disappointments, to use Freddie's polite parlance. I had been far enough along in the second instance to know I'd lost the son Freddie had longed for.

"But our baby," St. Sevier said, climbing on the bed and scooting over, "would be the most marvelous baby ever born."

"So humble, St. Sevier." I let the matter drop, but course Hugh would want his own little bundle of hope and joy.

Or several little bundles. Something about that thought tried to germinate in my mind as St. Sevier began kissing me. I had missed him badly even when he'd been lounging a mere two picnic blankets away. I kissed him back with all the passion and longing in me and all the esteem and liking I felt for him.

He was a good, dear man and ever so patient with me—also marvelously skilled between the sheets. Whatever he'd been about with Daphne Jones could keep for discussion on another day, if it ever needed discussing at all.

I had taken my traveling desk into the conservatory for the morning, intent on catching up on my correspondence, when the light dragoons came upon me.

"We're invading," Millicent MacNeil announced. "The racket and bustle in the house is deafening. Who knew spring cleaning was such a loud undertaking?"

"We are also taking advantage of the absence of our menfolk," Daphne Jones added. "Why they must travel twenty miles for a view of the ocean is a mystery for the ages."

Kathleen O'Dea took the place beside me on the couch. "Patrick said something about meeting with factors. I suspect they will meet with more than a few tankards of ale, too, and reminisce with St. Sevier about the less genteel times."

"Or," Lady Rutland said, settling on the chaise, "they wanted to elude the occasion of a mass cleaning of the public rooms. I am not above tasking officers with rehanging portraits or positioning statuary. Papa always said those giving orders must be reminded from time to time of how it feels to take an order. Even Wellington was answerable to Parliament in certain regards."

Millicent fluffed her skirts. "Is Parliament answerable to anybody? I do not believe they are."

The other ladies groaned in unison. "Milly is a radical," Lady Rutland said. "Tommie despairs of her. Next, she'll be telling you the Americans had the right idea."

"We are better off without a lot of colonial ingrates," Daphne Jones pronounced as two footmen wheeled trolleys into our midst.

"Back to the library with you gentlemen," Lady Rutland said when the food was set out on the low table. "We will serve ourselves, and we are not to be disturbed."

They bowed and withdrew with the air of men consigned to digging latrines.

"They hate dusting the books," Kathleen O'Dea said, "though there are precious fewer to dust now than there were a year ago. The library feels so much lighter for not being cluttered with mildewed poetry."

"Farming pamphlets," Lady Rutland muttered, setting an epergne of sandwiches before me. "It's not as if we have acres of corn to harvest hereabouts. Lady Violet, you are among friends. Do not stand on ceremony, or you shall starve."

"Every woman for herself," Daphne said, passing me a plate. "Fix bayonets and charge!"

Without the gentlemen, the ladies were a merrier bunch than I had anticipated. They traded recipes for lightening freckles—Milly's grannie swore by rubbing cut potatoes on bare skin, Daphne's mama was a proponent of lemon juice applied at night.

"I gave up in Spain," Kathleen O'Dea said. "I wore bonnets without number and carried parasols from dawn to sunset, but the Iberian sun had its way with my complexion. Patrick said it only gave him more to adore about me."

"He would," Milly muttered, which occasioned general merriment, to my surprise. "I don't think Tommie would notice if I wore a sack on my head."

Lady Rutland considered a bite of melon wrapped in a thin slice of smoked ham. "That might depend on whether you wore anything else at the time."

I had no sisters and had gone straight from daughter to wife without ever traversing the treacherous terrain of the single, available female out in Society. My sense as an observer was that young women competing for husbands had found the Mayfair Season a battleground.

As I listened to the ladies teasing each other and gently poking fun at their menfolk, I wondered if a young lady's come out wasn't instead an opportunity to form lifelong alliances and make friends. If army life could create that camaraderie even in an atmosphere defined by rank, why couldn't a Mayfair ballroom?

Daphne Jones held a plate of crumpets out to me. "St. Sevier notices what Lady Violet wears. That raspberry evening gown earned you many an appreciative glance, my lady."

"Such a color favors most women's complexions," I said, taking a crumpet, "and a satin-covered corset never hurt the drape of good fabric either."

This admission earned me a hoot from Millicent and a smiling *tsk, tsk* from Kathleen, while Lady Rutland shook her head. I had passed some sort of test with my rejoinder, though what exactly had Daphne Jones been asking me, and why had she stolen a moment in St. Sevier's arms where she was not assured of privacy?

That question bothered me as a pesky housefly will insist, in a dwelling the size of the Wood, on bothering the sole person attempting to practice her scales at the only piano on the premises.

"Will you write to dear Felix while you're here?" Lady Rutland asked as we devoured an unladylike number of profiteroles. "You must give him our warmest regards."

"I will write to Katie *and* Felix," I said. "It's very odd to think he's taken a wife, but nearly impossible to think of Felix now without his Katie. He is sorely smitten, to the point that he told Derwent to go to Coventry when Papa tried to meddle between the affianced parties."

That bordered on sharing family business, but such was the informality of the meal that I felt comfortable making the disclosure. The ladies were clearly fond of Felix, as was I. Katie's regard for her husband approached the nearer reaches of celestial adoration.

"The general did not favor my match with Damien," Lady Rutland said. "Mama wasn't too keen on Damien either, but she knew the Rutland heir was consumptive."

"Consumptive heirs can yet sire children," Kathleen said, swiping her finger through the cream of her profiterole.

Lady Rutland took a profiterole for herself. "Papa wanted me to marry a man whose first allegiance was to the military rather than to the land. He said any country has farmers to grow crops and livestock, but true patriots were to be found only in the military."

Daphne wrinkled her nose and chose another treat from the diminishing number on the tray. "Patriots? Half the enlisted men were avoiding marriage to the women they'd got with child. The other half were facing misdemeanor charges."

"Half the English recruits maybe," Millicent interjected. "In Scotland, the weaving trade collapsed, and the clearances left many a decent crofter no other choice but to take the king's shilling."

"In any case," Lady Rutland said, "I had seen what Mama endured, and knew of all men, I did not want the career officer for a husband. I have never regretted the decision to accept Rutland's suit."

An odd look passed between the ladies, a little sad, a little humorous. Kathleen O'Dea, who'd disported with Rutland in this very location, shared in the look to the same extent the others did. Was it possible she and Lady Rutland had reached some sort of accommodation where Rutland's amours were concerned?

My only frame of reference for that inquiry was the discussion I'd had with Freddie's mistress following his death. She had not sought his exclusive attention, but she'd been the only woman under his protection at the time, myself excepted.

She had approached me both to return some personal effects Freddie had been wearing when he'd expired—a pocket watch, a signet ring, sapphire sleeve buttons, and a sapphire cravat pin—and also to present me with bills for sums owed to her for services rendered.

When she had resolved matters that could have been handled by correspondence, she'd alerted me to the existence of Freddie's daughter. My reaction had been an odd sense of shared purpose, that we women were left to clean up after the man who'd cut such a wide and self-interested swath through both of our lives.

That same sense, of common gender uniting when it might have otherwise divided, permeated the moments following Lady Rutland's affirmation of appreciation for her husband. The ladies had made their choices and would stand by them, at least in public.

"I daresay Rutland has never regretted offering for you," Millicent observed. "And if he ever does, we will deal severely with him." Her threat was threaded with as much dire intent as humor, which I also found interesting.

In the course of this conversation, a day that had been blustery began to rain in earnest. In the south, a rainy day was usually simply wet and dreary. Here, hints of a storm came along with the precipitation. The wind had picked up, the wet spattered against the panes of the conservatory in increasingly loud volleys, and the space we occupied took on a chill.

"I ought to collect a shawl," I said, dusting my hands when I'd finished the last profiterole I would permit myself. "I am only halfway through my correspondence and can finish up in my sitting room." Where, I hoped, a fire had been laid and lit.

"I have account books to see to," Millicent said.

"Darning," Daphne added, getting to her feet. "I swear Garth goes through stockings as quickly as an infantryman on the march."

"While I will sleep off a fine meal," Kathleen said. "Lady Violet, where are you going?"

I stopped, writing desk in hand. "Back to the manor?"

"In this weather, we'll use the tunnel," Lady Rutland said, heading off in the opposite direction from whence she'd arrived. "The staff dislikes it when we encroach on their domain, but the tunnels are not exclusively for their convenience."

Well, of course. In all my wanderings around the property, I'd seen no grooms coming in from the stables for their noon meal, no laundresses traveling between the springhouse and the manor. Foot traffic of that nature disturbed the peace and beauty of the grounds, and tunnels were the answer.

On some older estates, the tunnels were Jacobite artifacts or relics of the coastal trade. More often, they were simply a means of keeping staff out of sight and—coincidentally—out of the wet.

Derwent Hall, my girlhood home, had a tunnel between the manor and the stable, as well as some subcellars no longer in use.

The tunnel from the conservatory was whitewashed and arched, with lit sconces at regular intervals and a smooth, well-swept brick floor. Two other tunnels intersected it, leading I knew not where, but those were also clean and well lit.

More effort and expense.

We emerged into the pantries outside the manor's kitchen and took the main steps into the foyer. The contrast between the informality of the conservatory, the utilitarian passages, and the foyer's chilly grandeur struck me as a metaphor for the challenges of managing a vast estate.

"Until dinner," Daphne Jones said, bobbing a curtsey.

Kathleen offered me the same courtesy, yawning behind her hand as she drifted off. Millicent bussed my cheek.

"We take getting used to," she said, "but I think you would have made a fine officer's wife." She bustled away after offering that high praise, presumably to see to her ledgers.

"You should be honored," Lady Rutland said. "For all her friendliness, Milly is sparing with approbation. You could use the escritoire in my private parlor to finish your letters, my lady. The fire is always lit in there, and the light is good."

"I am running out of ink, to be honest. The loan of some would be appreciated."

"You must make free with my supplies." Lady Rutland marched off down the corridor, and I, like a good little recruit, fell in step behind her. "When Rutland first mustered out, I was desperate to maintain my ties with other officers' wives. As the years have gone on, there is less and less to write about and fewer and fewer people to write to. I feel sometimes as if the Wood is a different world from the one I grew up in, much less exciting, but wonderfully peaceful and small."

"You don't regret missing the London whirl?"

"Heavens no. I had no idea there was London whirl to miss. Daphne is the restless one among us—her sister married a viscount's heir and is always inviting her to visit in the south—and you mustn't mind if she shows more than a passing interest in St. Sevier. They were close at one point, good friends and allies."

"Were they more than friends?" I would not have asked that question before luncheon. Hugh had assured me he had no former lovers among the ladies at the Wood, and I believed him. I also know, however, from my former association with Sebastian MacHeath, that one could be particularly fond of a member of the opposite sex without any expectation of becoming physically intimate.

"More than friends?" Lady Rutland mused. "Possibly. Viewed from the outside, the military looks like a lot of rules, regulations, and inviolable traditions. Men are flogged for neglecting to cut their hair, because order in the ranks rules over all other considerations. In reality, soldiers of every rank are human beings coping with a very hard job. They seek comfort in places that would appall polite society, and that is simply part of the cost of maintaining a fighting force."

She paused outside the parlor door. "Daphne is devoted to Garth, and St. Sevier is quite smitten with you. You need not trouble yourself over ancient history now."

I hadn't been, exactly. I had wanted to know St. Sevier's past simply because that was part of knowing him.

"Heaven defend us." Lady Rutland had stopped right inside the parlor door. "The general has taken a tumble. Lady Violet, please ring the bell-pull twice."

A portrait of an officer amid smoke and fighting sat at an odd angle against the corner of the sideboard. Lady Rutland struggled with the heavy frame, but managed to get it leaning upright against the sideboard leg. I had seen this picture properly hanging over the sideboard on my tour of the house.

The dashing officer was still pointing at the melee in the distance, and smoke still billowed from cannon and rifle barrels alike, but the sky above the battle had been rent with a long scratch through the paint.

"That can be repaired," I said, tugging the bell-pull. "I am certain that can be repaired."

Her ladyship straightened, her cameo-perfect features arranged in a thunderous frown. "Oh, eventually, I'm sure it can, but this is a Reynolds, one of the last Sir Joshua did, painted when Papa made colonel. Not just anybody will repair it. I told the footmen most specifically to be careful when they dusted and rehung it."

She retrieved a bottle of ink from the escritoire and passed it to me. "Perhaps you'd best use your sitting room after all, Lady Violet. I have some inquiries to make among the staff."

I took the bottle of ink with me upstairs, having no wish to observe as her ladyship convened her domestic court-martial.

CHAPTER SEVEN

"Was your day truly spent enjoying the sea air?" I asked, turning so St. Sevier could start on my hooks. He was in his shirtsleeves, his boots already exchanged for a pair of house slippers.

"That and shivering." He kissed my nape, which inspired a shiver of the delectable variety. "Rutland is doubly disadvantaged by having been the spare, and thus not raised to manage this parcel of land, and by having chosen the military, which can leave a man fit for little else." St. Sevier worked his way down my hooks, his touch light. "Rutland has no inroads with the trades, no connections beyond those he formed among other officers. His family tended its acres here in Cumbria and did not forge significant alliances in either commercial or aristocratic circles."

St. Sevier slipped his arms around my waist when he'd undone the last hook. "I am tired, Violet."

"You do not refer to the fatigue of a day spent racketing about in a coach with four other men." A day made longer by one of the coach wheels coming loose. The problem had been discovered before the wheel had actually flown from the axle, but the result had been a considerable delay on the homeward journey.

"MacNeil mostly rode on the box," St. Sevier said. "He spends a fair amount of time in Rutland's company and wasn't keen on being crammed into a coach with him all day. The coachman is Scottish, and I gather he and MacNeil shared more than a wee nip."

"You found the whole business tiresome, just as you found the military itself tiresome, but a fine place to practice medicine."

St. Sevier slipped his arms from my waist and ambled away. "True, and I am tired of being a guest. First in Scotland, now here. As a Frenchman, I will always be something of a guest in England, and in your bed..."

He withdrew his cravat pin and tossed it onto the vanity. The gesture had an edge, for St. Sevier preferred to own a few lovely possessions that he treasured rather than many for which he cared little. His cravat pins might well be mementos from relatives buried in France, or purchased from some émigré in London.

Rather than fall into the routine of undressing St. Sevier, I remained where I was, my dress undone.

"In point of fact," I said, "I am a visitor in your bed, not the other way around."

"Rutland asked if I was courting you," St. Sevier replied. "I did not know what to say. You have given me permission to pay you my addresses, and you are all that is passionate in bed, and yet... You come so close and no closer, Violet. I feel it here." He thumped his chest lightly with his fist.

"No man has come as close to me as you have, St. Sevier." Sebastian MacHeath and I had been best friends, as young people can be, but not as a male and female share intimacy in adulthood.

St. Sevier met my gaze in the cheval mirror as he untied his cravat. "What of your sainted husband?"

"I was an ornament to Freddie, a pampered broodmare who could not fulfill my purpose. He was never in love with me and frankly discouraged me from falling in love with him. *Not the done thing.*"

"I hate him," St. Sevier said, prowling closer and sounding very

French. "You terrified him, and he was a boor, and I rejoice that he met an early end."

I had never, ever been afraid of St. Sevier, but his tone reminded me that he'd been to war, lost much, and had a temper all the more impressive for being cold.

"You are in a mood, sir."

He stood near enough that I caught his honeysuckle fragrance, near enough that I could see the fatigue in his eyes. "Daphne Jones made subtle advances to me of an arguably inappropriate nature. Why would she do this?"

"Because you are handsome, charming, and a man she was close to in her past?"

St. Sevier reached behind me and undid the clasp of my necklace. "She and I were not close as lovers are close. She spent a great deal of time in the infirmary, true, but I suspect her purpose was to see her husband promoted. Jones had purchased the lowliest of commissions—a mere cornet—and his best hope for advancement was a field promotion. That and they had no children, so she had time on her hands."

St. Sevier trailed the pendant slowly along my décolletage.

"Perhaps she harbored a tendresse for you, and you were oblivious to the attraction?"

He desisted and set the pendant on the vanity. "A man is never oblivious to a woman's regard for him."

Male arrogance had no nationality. "But you did not see her overture in the offing, and are not absolutely sure it was an overture, are you?"

He slipped one sleeve button free, then the other. "Touché, darling Violet. How was your day with the ladies?"

I had scored a hit, for St. Sevier's change of subject was anything but deft. "They are different when the tomcats are away." I took a seat on the vanity stool, collected my skirts, and bent to untie my garters.

I rolled down my stockings, glad to be peeling out of my finery.

The day had been long, with dinner pushed back to accommodate the delay in the return of the menfolk. The weather had not improved, and thus the damp chill of spring required fires that did not quite leave a body warm.

"Rutland is taken with you," St. Sevier said, watching me remove my stockings. "I believe that was the point behind his question. If I am merely your escort, he will make overtures. If you have shown me a suitor's favor, you are safe from his attentions."

"You have brooded on this. Help me get my dress off." Between us, we lifted the fabric over my head, then dealt with my stays. St. Sevier passed me his dressing gown—how I loved wearing his scent, even if the hem nearly dragged on the floor—and gave me first crack behind the privacy screen.

The moment did not feel right to tell St. Sevier that Rutland had also approached me regarding St. Sevier's status, but in hindsight, Rutland's question had been awkward at best.

"How are the ladies different when their husbands are away?" St. Sevier asked when I sat to take down my hair.

"They are more in charity with each other, more 'we ladies' while the husbands are a collective challenge rather than precious individual spouses to be guarded against all perils. If Lady Rutland knows his lordship is straying, she truly isn't much worried about it, and Rutland certainly professes his regard for her regularly."

St. Sevier took up a perch, cross-legged, in the middle of the bed. He put me in mind of those cats in Daphne Jones's parlor. Watchful, elegant, entirely self-contained.

"You are not impressed with his lordship's avowals of devotion?"

My hair was in a simple coronet, easy to undo. "Of course not. We saw him with Mrs. O'Dea, did we not? Now you tell me he's sniffing about my skirts. I do believe we might have to cut our visit short, St. Sevier."

"But you are loath to return to London."

"I am. Nigh dreading it. Daphne Jones had best hope she's never widowed. If she's bored with her circumstances here, surrounded by friends, with a household to run and beautiful countryside to enjoy, mourning will drive her utterly barmy."

I was apparently not to enjoy Hugh's attention to my hair. I undid the ribbons and plaits and took up his brush as he left the bed.

"Violet, why won't you ask me?"

"Ask you?"

"Ask me for so simple a thing as to tend to your hair, which you know I enjoy." He gently pried the brush from my hand. "You are the sweetest, most maddening woman I have ever had the pleasure to know."

We were both in a mood, apparently, because now that he was brushing out and rebraiding my hair, I was impatient with him. I had not asked, he had not offered. What point was I trying to make by not asking, or what point was he trying to make by not offering?

"Something is amiss at the Wood," I said. "Something besides a commanding officer with no knack for dealing with the trades, or a quartet of marriages showing a bit of wear."

"Jones said something to that effect when the coach wheel came loose." St. Sevier tied off my braid with a green ribbon and treated me to a firm hug about the shoulders. "Something along the lines of 'what next?' And 'where will it end?' O'Dea, garrulous by nature, was uncharacteristically silent. I thought Jones was merely referring to a day of bad roads, worse weather, and an ill-timed mishap with a coach wheel."

"Perhaps he and Mrs. Jones have a reason to be on the outs with each other? Jones is reported to be a favorite with Lady Rutland."

St. Sevier offered me a hand up, a courtly gesture more in keeping with our usual dealings. "Then Daphne accosts me on the garden path. Perhaps she was trying to make Jones jealous."

I would have gone straight to the bed and wielded the warmer on the sheets, but St. Sevier stopped me by pulling me in close.

"I did not anticipate what being around these people... the challenge this visit would entail. Please be patient with me, Violet."

I stroked his hair, wondering what demons haunted his memory beyond those I already knew about. "They seem to be a gracious four-some of couples friendly from long acquaintance and shared experience, but there's money trouble here, marital trouble, staff trouble... The Wood should be a jewel of bucolic contentment. The longer we stay, the more it feels exactly as you describe army life—a combination of drama and boredom, petty displays, and grand tragedy. I do not want to return to London, St. Sevier, but I want to be away from this place."

He kissed my cheek. "Return to bed with me. I missed you, Violet. All day, watching the dreary countryside go by, listening to stories I've heard a half-dozen times before, admiring the sea, which looks quite the same as it always has on dreary days, and trying to ignore the cold, I missed you."

I sank into his embrace, feeling as if we had finally restored our balance with each other. "I missed you, too, terribly. Tomorrow, we must contrive a way to avoid the company of our hosts and read some poetry to each other."

"I will make poetry with you in that bed, my lady."

He was better than his word, for my need of him had an edge of desperation. To me, the couples at the Wood were a cautionary tale, composed of casual infidelity, disrespected vows, and ignored needs. Lady Rutland's declaration at luncheon troubled me in particular.

She claimed to have never regretted her choice of husband, and her friends had heartily seconded her sentiments.

I did not. She'd married a man who wasn't managing his household well, who had apparently expressed a passing interest in cavorting with a guest under his own roof, and who was already trifling with an employee's wife. I could not imagine a fellow I'd be less inclined to marry.

Rutland and Freddie would have got along famously.

Those reflections reminded me what a treasure I had in St. Sevier, and while I would make no declarations, I could show him with my ardor how very much he meant to me.

I awoke before daybreak, intent on returning to my own bed when a sound stopped me. "What is that?"

St. Sevier, tousled and naked, lay beside me. "Coffee."

He posited the hope that his morning tray would have already been set out in the sitting room, which didn't seem likely as the sun was not yet up, and cold coffee was an abomination against decency.

The sound came again. "That," I said, rising and wrapping St. Sevier's dressing gown around me. I opened a window and saw the source of the noise. "There are sheep in the garden."

"Cheaper than hiring men to scythe. *Is* there any coffee?" Such longing colored that question. "Even tea would be a mercy."

I left the window and peeked into the sitting room. "None yet. Shall I ring?"

"I entreat you, if you must persist in attempting to converse with me at this ungodly English hour, ring for a tray."

The hour wasn't that ungodly. I tugged the bell-pull and returned to the window, where the predawn illumination showed not merely a few sheep turned loose to nibble the verges of the walkways, but an entire herd of freshly shorn ewes and lambs.

"This cannot be right." A precocious youngster leaped onto a bench near my window, bleating merrily to his fellows. Sheep were particularly casual about defecation. Unlike a horse or cow, which would often stop all forward progress to tend to nature's call with straining and profuse groaning, a sheep simply lifted its tail—or what remained of its tail—as it grazed or strolled along.

The lamb on the bench indulged in nature's urge, then hopped down and went gamboling on its way.

"Lord Rutland will have an apoplexy."

St. Sevier rolled to his side and wrapped his arms around my pillow. "I am having an apoplexy for want of coffee. Come back to bed and distract me from my affliction."

"Alas, for your *affliction*, I must away."

He peered under the covers. "My affliction is mighty, Violet. Other than coffee, I can think of only one balm sufficient to soothe such distress."

The sheep nearest the window resumed bleating. "The household will soon be in an uproar. Those sheep are not supposed to be in the garden, trampling manicured beds and leaving manure on benches."

St. Sevier rose and strolled to the window, wearing not one stitch and imposing on me the sight of a handsome man sporting a grand case of procreative readiness.

"*Bon Dieu*, a biblical plague of sheep. Rutland will soon muster the troops, and somebody will be court-martialed at full volume."

I shrugged out of his dressing gown, tugged my dress on over my chemise, and gathered up the rest of my clothing. "I'd best be off before the gardens are full of curious eyes." I kissed St. Sevier—only that—and took a moment to memorize the sight of him—untidy, undressed, aroused, and delectable.

"I miss you already," I said. "See you at breakfast."

"Breakfast should be interesting." He patted my bottom as I hurried off to the balcony doors, and that small gesture of familiarity and affection fortified me as much as all our intimacies from the previous evening.

I had barely managed to toss off my dress, turn down my own covers, and lay my head on the pillow when Lucy tapped on my door.

"Come in," I replied, trying to sound sleepy and probably failing.

"Lawks-a-mercy, milady, the house has run mad." Lucy carried a tray and kicked the door closed behind her. "Sheep in the garden and Lord Rutland calling for blood. You'd think somebody tried to assassinate the king."

"Somebody left a gate open," I said, sitting up. "Is that truly a serious offense?"

Lucy set down the tray and went to the window. "They are wrecking the flower beds. Rutland sets a powerful store by his posies."

Or by the appearance of affluence they created? I rose and donned my own dressing gown. "That sounds like a lot of sheep."

In my dressing gown, I ventured to the corner of the balcony overlooking the garden. A half-dozen gardeners were trying to herd the beasts out the back gate, but the sheep were disinclined to be herded. Then too, gardeners were not shepherds or sheep dogs, to have the knack of coaxing the animals in the desired direction was not in evidence.

"Here comes the army," Lucy muttered at my side as Colonel Lord Rutland strode onto the terrace.

His lordship turned a simple job into a rout—with victory to the sheep. They dodged every which way, trotted up and down the paths, cut across the flower beds, and made sport of the fountain like a herd of naughty schoolboys.

I waved. "My lord, good morning!"

Gone was the suave host, the urbane officer. Rutland's complexion rivaled the red tulips still standing, and his expression promised summary execution to the nearest ovine.

"My lady, now is not the time for idle chatter."

"Call for the shepherds to bring in a pair of collies," I yelled down. "You're making the damage worse with all this chasing around."

He strode off with a wave, and a quarter hour of mayhem ensued until a consultation with MacNeil and O'Dea apparently resulted in the same advice. The requisite canine expertise was brought to bear on the problem. The sheep quit the field with good grace thereafter, trotting through the open back gates as Lucy and I watched from our balcony.

"More fun than a championship cricket match," Lucy observed, swatting the pillows on my bed into place. "I have never heard such a lot of profanity over nothing. Sheep ain't stupid, but I have my doubts about those men."

"Lord Rutland is not exactly a man of the land."

"Neither are you, but you knew enough to send for the shepherds."

"His lordship was upset."

"Over a lot of bleating sheep? They would have left eventually. There's little enough for 'em to eat in the garden."

True enough. "Which suggests they did not wander in on their own. I had best get down to breakfast, Lucy. Round two of the cricket championship is doubtless getting under way as I speak."

I could hear the arguing before I'd crossed the foyer, Thomas MacNeil's burr resounding down the corridor.

"Ye make too much of a minor mishap, my lord!"

"The cost of those tulip bulbs is not minor," Rutland retorted. "The labor needed to plant them in the first place, the effort now required to restore the beds, the cleaning... The damned sheep ate every low-hanging blossom from the plum trees along the fruit wall, and that is more expense."

I sidled into the breakfast parlor, coming upon a tableau I knew all too well. The lord of the manor sat at the head of the table decrying in full voice a situation that did not merit shouting. Reasonable people tried to convince him of that, while he grew only more upset. My own father excelled at breakfast-table drama, which I had learned to ignore before I put up my hair.

"So we have less of the plum preserves," MacNeil shot back. "That is not a tragedy, and we have the help on hand to clean up the garden easily enough now that shearing is over."

Lady Rutland had developed a compelling fascination with her eggs. Milly MacNeil was similarly absorbed in studying her tea. St. Sevier was doubtless still occupied worshipping his pot of coffee—or soothing his affliction—while I was hungry.

"You have thriving lavender borders, my lord," I said, taking a plate and helping myself to ham and eggs. "Thin them and replant half the tulip beds with lavender, which can be sold, used domestically for soaps and sachets, and put to good use in the herbal. Tulips afford a few weeks of color, but they are useless the rest of the year and require lifting and replanting."

MacNeil and Rutland looked at me as if I'd burst out singing "La Marseillaise."

"Good morning, your ladyship," Rutland said, rising and sketching me a bow. MacNeil did likewise, and Lady Rutland tried for a smile.

"Are you a gardener," his lordship asked, "to make such a suggestion?" He could not dismiss me for insubordination, but he could lard his words with disdain.

I would not have fared very well in the military, apparently.

"I grew up in the south," I said, taking a seat opposite Millicent, "on a large, old-fashioned estate. No Englishwoman raised in the country is entirely ignorant of how to maintain a garden. The Wood shows to excellent advantage, but thanks to the untimely intervention of your sheep, you have a chance to rethink your gardening strategy. Tulips are an extravagance, and in my experience, they make more of an impact as an accent than when deployed in uniform platoons."

"She's saying," MacNeil muttered, "that a few good snipers will be more effective than all the marching nitwits the recruiting sergeants send us, be their uniforms ever so new."

Millicent passed me the teapot. "Might you sketch a few ideas for us, Lady Violet?"

"Of course, and I will be happy to help thin and transplant the lavender. Autumn would have served better, but early spring can work as well."

Lady Rutland set the toast rack by my elbow, followed by the butter dish. "You garden? You personally garden?"

"I do. Quite gratifying to bring order to a patch of ground and enjoy the fruits of one's own labor and imagination."

"That's all very well," Rutland said, "but Bevins will have to be sacked. Leaving the gates open at night is the very definition of dereliction of duty."

Bevins—the name brought to mind an older fellow wearing a patch over one eye.

"Ye canna sack a man with only the one good eye," MacNeil shot back. "Maybe he needs an assistant."

"He *is* an assistant," Rutland retorted. "What sort of undergardener is kept on after an incident like this?"

My eggs were not as hot as I preferred them, but then, the company wasn't as congenial as I preferred either.

"Bevins could have left every garden gate wide open, and the sheep would still not have found their way to the tulips unassisted," I said, buttering my toast.

Rutland glowered down his nose at me. My papa had perfected the same look, to the point that my brothers took turns amusing one another imitating him.

"The sheep are at spring grass, my lord. Their pastures have never appealed to them more strongly. By contrast, your tulips hold no interest for them, and if you inquire, you will likely find the back gate was closed up behind them."

"Closed," MacNeil said, "but the latch did not catch, such as might happen if somebody was careless."

I drizzled honey into my tea, watching the golden skein slow to a few drips. "You are implying the gate was wide open as a result of Bevins's neglect. The sheep then by dark of night—when sheep are less prone to wander lest predators be at large—broke out of their pasture across the park all on their own, chose to collect in the garden rather than graze the park, and then the wind conveniently blew the gate *almost shut* behind them?"

Lady Rutland aimed a look at her spouse down the breakfast table. "Lady Violet raises interesting points."

"I suspect," I said, stirring my tea, "Bevins's record is exemplary up until now. Before he's drummed out of the corps, should he not at least be interviewed?"

"He should." That from MacNeil. "We should also examine the gate between the sheep pasture and the park."

"That will be firmly latched," I suggested, "lest the sheep wander back through to their home pasture should the garden gate conveniently blow open again. Might I have a jam tart?"

The tray had reposed by Lord Rutland's plate. He sent it around to me by way of Millicent. "We'll investigate, starting with a thorough interrogation of the relevant suspects. Ladies, I wish you a pleasant day in the garden." He rose and marched out, heels rapping against the carpets.

"We have our orders," I said, offering a mock salute in the direction of the doorway, and where was St. Sevier when a lady needed cheerful breakfast conversation?

"And I have mine," MacNeil said, rising. "I'd best find Bevins before his lordship does. Ladies, I apologize for unpleasantness at table. We'll get to the bottom of this."

He followed in his lordship's wake, leaving an awkward silence behind.

"But what will we find when we do?" I mused. "Terrorizing a garden with errant sheep is an odd sort of mischief. What would such a prank accomplish?"

"Who knows?" Lady Rutland said. "But I haven't seen his lordship this fired up since his favorite gelding got loose on the morning of a parade inspection."

Worked up indeed—and over a few trampled beds of tulips?

The next three days saw one mishap after another, while Lord Rutland went from bellicose to blustering to brooding. The men tiptoed around him. The ladies carried on with a forced good cheer that had doubtless served them well when battle with Napoleon's forces approached.

After the ladies had retired from the dinner table, their good cheer vanished, replaced by a mood both weary and tense.

"Bevins did himself no favors choosing now to travel down to

Liverpool," Lady Rutland observed as a footman wheeled a tea cart into the family parlor.

"He always goes to see his sister in the spring," Kathleen O'Dea replied, settling onto the sofa. "Patrick has been talking about a trip to Ireland to see his granny, once the garden crops are in."

Daphne Jones took the place beside her. "How long would you be gone?"

Millicent stood by the window, looking out into darkness, her back to us. "Would you come back?"

Lady Rutland began pouring out and passed the first cup to Kathleen. "If Patrick leaves Kathleen here at the Wood, he'll return for her. Patrick likes his diversions, but he's a loyal sort. Witness his proposed visit to see his granny."

"He's only at the idle-talk stage," Kathleen said, adding a spoon to the saucer. "Lady Violet, you take a drop of honey, I believe?"

"That will do, and no shortbread for me." The meal had been long and strained—again—and I was eager to seek my bed.

Or St. Sevier's bed.

"Bevins did not tamper with a coach wheel," I said. "Bevins did not scratch the brigadier's portrait. Bevins did not sour an entire batch of sweet cream." That last "mishap" had occurred after Bevins's departure. He'd decamped for the south at midafternoon on the day previous to the great sheep invasion, if the accounts of his fellow gardeners could be believed.

But why start a substantial journey at midafternoon?

"Cream goes off," Lady Rutland said tiredly.

Not the evening after it was drawn, it didn't, not if it was properly chilled in the springhouse and stored on ice.

"Cook smelled vinegar," Millicent retorted, abandoning her post by the window and taking the place beside Lady Rutland. "The cream was purposely soured. I will take all the shortbread Lady Violet declines."

"You should be making a list of incidents," I said. "When they occurred and who was in a position to perpetrate them. There's the cream, the coach wheel, the sheep, the portrait—"

"The scorch marks on the curtains in the servants' hall," Kathleen added. "The broken figurines in the formal parlor, the dent in the piano in the ballroom."

Lady Rutland set down the teapot. "The dent happened before the Yuletide holidays. Surely an accident as the ballroom was prepared for the annual open house?"

"Will you leave it to the menfolk to sort this out?" I asked. "St. Sevier tells me that Bevins can't see well by daylight and has even less vision at night, and yet, Lord Rutland accused Bevins first when anybody on the grounds could have fetched a bucket of oats and led the bellwether astray."

Lady Rutland had forgotten to pour herself a cup of tea, or perhaps she didn't care for any. "You are sure of that? That Bevins cannot see well?"

"If I were ever to trust any opinion from anywhere in the entire medical pantheon, I would trust St. Sevier's."

A volley of glances ricocheted around the room, as obvious as gunfire.

Lady Rutland led the charge. "What else does St. Sevier say?"

"He agrees with me that the pattern is one of petty annoyances rather than outright criminal intent. A few trampled tulips are an inconvenience. A pair of gamboling dogs can do the same sort of damage. A portrait with a scratch through the sky can be repaired. Curtains in the servants' hall with a few scorch marks still block the sun and provide privacy."

"A loose coach wheel is dangerous." Daphne Jones spoke with particular fierceness. "Our husbands were *all* in that coach, and the terrain hereabouts is hilly."

"Rutland could have broken his neck," Athena murmured. "I could not have borne for him to spend years facing down Boney's cannon only to die on a Cumbrian hillside."

Millicent gave her a one-armed hug. "We none of us could."

"Will you then," I said, "leave it to the menfolk to bluster and curse on their own, or will you make a serious effort to aid them? Who has access to the carriage house? Are the coaches regularly maintained, and was this coach overdue for a trip to the smithy? Could the loose wheel have been merely an accident, while all the other incidents were intentional mischief?"

I had risen to pace at some point in this digression, and four women watched me as if I might produce a loaded firearm from my skirt pockets.

"I could ask Rutland," Lady Rutland said. "I don't know as the vehicles are on a maintenance schedule."

"I can ask Tommie," Millicent murmured. "In private, lest he think I'm criticizing him, though house matters keep him more than busy, and the stables are not part of his remit."

"Is the carriage house locked?" I went on. "If so, where is the key kept, and who has access to it? How exactly does one loosen a coach wheel such that it doesn't wobble until miles after the tampering has occurred, if in fact there was tampering?"

"Garth will know." Daphne scooted a bit forward on her seat cushion. "He has a mechanical mind. Should have been an artificer. You truly think the coach wheel might have been an accident, Lady Violet?"

"I don't know, but most of the trouble has been domestic—the scorch marks, the cream gone off, the broken figurines, the scratched portrait—until we get to the sheep. Even that wasn't perpetrated on some tenant property, but right in the formal gardens next to the manor."

"Rutland took it as a direct slap in the face," Lady Rutland said quietly. "He's brooding. Rutland never broods. He decides on a course of action and it's 'eyes front, forward march' until the objective is secured."

"That is the perishing truth," Millicent muttered, half smiling. The other ladies joined her reluctant humor, doubtless calling upon years of living under Rutland's command.

"He cannot march his way through this contretemps," I said. "The female staff will tell him nothing, and it's upon them that responsibility for broken figurines, soured cream, and scorched curtains must fall."

"Or appear to fall," Kathleen said, taking a piece of shortbread from Millicent's plate. "The portrait, the sheep, the dented piano, the coach wheel... Those incidents cast suspicion upon the male staff, and they won't be forthcoming with Rutland either."

"Aren't we making too much of a lot of nothing?" Lady Rutland asked. "If the coach wheel was merely a mishap, then the rest amounts to incompetence, slacking, and pranks. Nothing that word of a French advance wouldn't put a stop to."

"Pity," Daphne said, "we haven't any French armies to fight at present."

Before anybody could respond to that extraordinary sentiment, the gentlemen joined us. Rutland drew his chair up next to mine, while St. Sevier sat with the ladies on the sofa. O'Dea lounged on the sofa arm next to his wife, while Jones brought over the chair from behind the escritoire to sit near Lady Rutland.

Tommie MacNeil appointed himself quartermaster of the decanters and had soon served a nightcap to each of the gentlemen as well as to Millicent and Kathleen.

"To those fallen in battle," Tommie said, raising his glass. "May their memories forever redound to the glory of the realm."

St. Sevier took a polite sip and raised his glass again. "To those who survived the battles, may their sacrifices be appreciated by a grateful nation." I noticed that he did not specify which nation or nations he referred to.

So it went around the room, with Wellington's good health, the Sovereign, Blucher, and General Grossnickel all coming in for good wishes. The lot of us were dithering, making excuses to avoid the topic foremost on all of our minds.

An awkward silence rose after the toast to Lady Rutland's esteemed father. Lady Rutland as hostess should have started the conversation down some pleasant, agreeable road, but I lacked the self-restraint to allow that.

"You need an inspector general," I said. "Somebody not from the estate who has the skills and standing to investigate all that is going on here. As Lord Rutland has pointed out, petty mishaps are taking an increasing toll on the Wood's coffers, staff morale is suffering, and I daresay even the officer corps would like some answers."

"Hear, hear," Patrick O'Dea said, raising his glass slightly. "If the potted morning glories had been set out in the garden, we could have lost a dozen lambs in the course of a night. The morning glories were on the schedule, but then we had the nasty weather, and I said they should bide another week in the conservatory."

Rutland held up his glass, and MacNeil provided the refill. "Why haven't you mentioned this earlier, O'Dea?"

"Didn't occur to me, but one of the undergardeners—old Chernow—mentioned it when we took stock today of what remains in the conservatory. I realized the same is true had the beasts got to grazing on the ivy or the yew hedges."

"Those plants are all poisonous to sheep?" Lady Rutland asked.

"Irises aren't good for them either," I replied. "Acorns, ferns, holly berries are also dangerous to livestock."

The company looked at me as one, making me very aware again that I'd had a rural upbringing among mostly male family. My father had regularly come to table worried about a tup that had got loose and gone feasting among the ferns or taken a notion to nibble the ivy.

"You ladies," I said, "probably know more military history than most Oxford graduates. You dined on such fare for years. I know life on a rural estate."

Sr. Sevier was regarding me with a pensive expression, probably recalling my dread of returning to my London town house. I knew Town life, too, though it seemed a shallow undertaking compared to producing the raw materials that fed, clothed, and largely housed a nation. I also believed fresh air superior to coal smoke.

"We lost not a single lamb," Lady Rutland said, "and there could well be an innocent explanation for the whole business. Sheep are notorious for going astray, are they not? Perhaps we ought not to dwell on it. The hillwalkers will soon descend, and we will have all we can do tending the gardens and shipping the produce."

Her good cheer was taken up by the other ladies, while beside me, Rutland kept his peace and treated his subordinates to considering looks.

"You aren't buying it," I said quietly. "You think the trouble will continue."

"I can think of no reason why it would stop, my lady. When advancing through enemy territory, the worst thing an invading army can do is set up camp and make a target of itself."

"My lord, you are no longer at war."

His smile was wan. "Am I not? Somebody has begun an invasion, Lady Violet, but I am at a loss to say who, or why they have decided to cut up my peace."

His peace was cut up, while Bevins had nearly lost his livelihood on the strength of conjecture alone. Rutland knew more than he was saying, but just as the staff would not be forthcoming with him, he wasn't about to be forthcoming with me. I made my excuses shortly thereafter and asked St. Sevier to do me the courtesy of lighting me up to bed.

He complied with an alacrity bordering on desperation.

CHAPTER EIGHT

"They are obsessed with what is likely nothing more than unfortunate coincidence," St. Sevier said, pacing the bedroom in his shirtsleeves. "A porcelain shepherdess blown off the mantel when a window was left open has become proof of enemy snipers in the undergrowth."

"Porcelain is heavy, St. Sevier."

"Then a maid was clumsy when dusting, a footman not careful enough when taking a portrait down for cleaning. Rutland's answer to everything is to sack somebody, and MacNeil, O'Dea, and Jones are losing patience with him."

I had changed into my nightclothes, taken down my hair, and tended to my ablutions, while St. Sevier had muttered in a combination of French and English and paced like a caged panther.

"Rutland knows more than he's letting on," I said, taking the stool before the vanity. "Will you braid my hair for me?"

"Yes," St. Sevier said, striding across the room. "Yes, I will braid your gorgeous hair, and that will soothe my temper. Rutland wanted to sack Thaddeus Bevins without even speaking to the man. Bevins tramped through miles of mud, endured on bad rations for years, almost lost his eyesight and his arm for the glory of Good King George, and Rutland nearly turned him off without a character or notice."

I passed St. Sevier the brush. "Rutland will say the Wood is not an eleemosynary institution, and if Bevins has been negligent, he doesn't deserve his job."

My father would say the same thing, doubtless, but he would not sack a loyal retainer without severance, character, or warning. *Not the done thing.*

"When will Bevins return?" I asked.

"A week or so. This place seethes, Violet, like an army camp can seethe. While serving under Rutland, I treated much misery that had little to do with war itself. Wives suffering the ill effects of male tempers, men poisoned half to death by too much bad drink. Outbreaks of dysentery, measles, mumps, chicken pox, and worse."

He paused in his brushing, his gaze clearly on the past. "Rutland was recovering from a case of smallpox when I first arrived. The army itself began to strike me as an illness. Because the mission of defeating the Corsican was so desperate, much decency and civility were allowed to lapse."

"Isn't that military life in general? A hundred lashes for a missing button and so forth?"

St. Sevier resumed wielding the brush with a gentle touch. "Wellington exerted an odd blend of respect for tradition and basic pragmatism regarding military discipline. The typical English model of command was to ensure the enlisted men were more afraid of their superior officers than of the enemy. The German school of thought says an army should be forged along fraternal bonds, such that an honorable soldier would never leave his brothers-in-arms to fight on without him, irrespective of rank."

"That feels good. Felix has mentioned this topic in passing. Napoleon was very popular with his troops, wasn't he?"

"Some of them literally marched to and from Moscow in bare feet in the dead of winter for him. He made the French army the jewel in the empire's crown. Rewarded bravery and skill rather than allowing wealth to buy rank. Napoleon earned the respect of France's enemies. We needed that," St. Sevier added softly, "after the violence and confusion of the Terror. When the Austrians were poised to wipe France from the face of the earth, we needed the tonic Napoleon offered."

I was reminded of the ladies' earlier comments about a mutual enemy serving to unite troops who otherwise turned on one another. The tonic had come at the cost of hundreds of thousands of French lives, among countless other deaths, and now France was once again ruled by a king.

A topic for another day. "Do you suspect Rutland's lieutenants have turned on each other?"

St. Sevier set the brush aside and divided my hair into three skeins. "That is a possibility. MacNeil, as house steward, feels responsible for the chaos at the Wood itself. O'Dea, with authority over the grounds and gardens, has come in for some sharp questions from Rutland regarding the sheep and the coach wheel."

"And Jones, the junior officer with the unhappy wife? Is he also under suspicion?" Garth Jones was quiet, but as Rutland's man of business, he'd know the toll all this petty mischief was taking on Rutland's exchequer. As the junior officer, perhaps he had the loyalty of the staff to a greater extent than his lordship did.

"I have maintained my distance from Jones," St. Sevier said, plaiting my hair. "He looks at me like a man hatching a quarrel in his mind. I have no wish to be called out for the sake of his wounded pride."

A man on the outs with his own family, being made to feel guilty for the deaths of older siblings, and afflicted with a lonely wife might have many quarrels hatching in his mind.

"Jones seems quiet, but then, my father claims it's the quiet ones who bear watching."

St. Sevier tied off my braid and stood behind me. "Tomorrow, you and I will go riding, non? Wear your habit down to breakfast, and we

will get away from this place before the day's accusations and specu-
lations start."

I had thought to start my day making that list I'd mentioned to the
ladies—incidents, suspects, clues, that sort of thing.

"We might instead try speaking to some of the staff, St. Sevier.
Rutland will never be able to bully or command answers from his
own employees. He hasn't the knack. They are loyal to him, but I
doubt they trust him. They would be no more forthcoming with an
unfamiliar magistrate borrowed from the next county, so I didn't
suggest that."

And the mischief had to be the work of staff. Curdling sweet
cream required access to the dairy or the pantry. Scorching curtains
meant bringing a hot iron into the servants' hall or effecting the
damage while the curtains waited in the laundry to be rehung after a
washing. The broken figurines were found in the family parlor.

These were not public rooms, but rather, the working gears of the
estate. The only people with routine access other than the couples
dwelling at the Wood were the staff.

"The employees are legion, Violet. They will not chat openly
with some earl's daughter, or worse, a French doctor whom they do
not know."

"They know you. Bevins knew you, bad eyesight and all. He isn't
the only one, I'm sure, who would put his faith in you before he'd
repose it in any of the others."

I rose and wrapped my arms around St. Sevier before he could
start kissing me and distracting me.

"You are outraged that Rutland would suspect Bevins," I went
on, "and without even speaking to the man. I've seen others here who
are less than hale, St. Sevier. Another assistant gardener has a peg leg.
One of the gamekeepers is all but deaf and missing most of an ear.
The shepherd brought in to clear the sheep from the garden was
lacking a hand. You likely treated them all, and they survived the war
because of you."

He held me, his heartbeat a steady tattoo beneath my cheek. "I am no longer the medical authority for a regiment on the march. If I treated some wounds years ago, that is all in the past."

"You talk in your sleep," I said, easing away. "The past climbs into bed with us every night. If you leave here without seeing to it that the guilty and the innocent beneath Rutland's command are accurately sorted, you will add to your stock of nightmares."

He finished undressing by the firelight, disappeared behind the privacy screen, then banked the coals without donning so much as a dressing gown. The limited light gilded his lean frame and emphasized the shadows and hollows of his face while I waited beneath the covers.

"I want to leave this place," he said. "Worse is afoot here than broken porcelain and loose sheep. The ladies are unhappy, the men are uneasy, the staff is growing restive, and the commanding officer lacks the skill to resolve what's amiss. You are right that I do not want to turn my back on this situation, Violet, but neither do I relish the task of sorting out what has gone wrong."

"You need not sort through it alone," I said, patting the pillow. "And you need not sort through it now. We will ride out in the morning, make lists, and begin an investigation in earnest tomorrow."

He ambled to the bed and climbed in, spooning himself around me. "Or we could leave."

I was tempted to take him up on that offer, but then I thought of Bevins, so genuinely glad to see St. Sevier, and St. Sevier, feeling like a guest wherever he went.

"Nonsense. Your friends need you now, and I love a good intrigue."

"We should travel on, Violet. The whole situation will soon grow exceedingly messy."

How I loved his embrace, loved the warmth and comfort of cuddling up with him. "You know something."

"I know nothing. I heard Lady Rutland and Kathleen O'Dea arguing as I went down to dinner. They were most heated, and the words 'Ireland' and 'hopeless' were mentioned. Being a gentleman, I absented myself from the corridor before I overheard anything more."

"Patrick is thinking of making a trip to Ireland. Kathleen made a general announcement over the teapot, and Lady Rutland treated it as a case of first impression." Or had she? "You suspect O'Dea is leaving the scene of his crimes after taking petty revenge for Rutland's poaching?"

"I suspect I am alone behind a locked door with a lovely woman in my bed, and talk of intrigue and infidelity bores me."

"Part of you isn't bored," I noted, wigging my hips back into the curve of his body.

"All of me is certain we should depart from this place, Violet."

I took St. Sevier's hand and settled it over my breast. "Stubborn. I adore that about you. Things will look better in the morning. They always do."

I was soon flat on my back, enjoying a much-improved outlook on life—as I hope St. Sevier was—but my prognostication was wrong. Things did not look better in the morning *at all*.

"Lucy claims meals belowstairs have become dead silent," I said, surveying the saddle room. To all appearances, the space was tidy. Girths were draped over saddles, bridles hung neatly on pegs along the wall, each peg labeled with a horse's name.

My own father could not have asked for a more orderly arrangement of the gear necessary to outfit a horse for riding, and yet, somebody had wrought a subtle form of disarray.

"That's a snaffle bit, ye see?" an aging Yorkshireman in a groom's serviceable attire said. "But it's been buckled into old Hooky's bridle, and that gelding would no more heed a snaffle when he's on t' muscle than he'd attend to a butterfly on his arse, beggin' milady's pardon."

I was bursting with questions, but let St. Sevier manage the conversation.

"And tell me, Carruthers, are they are all rearranged?" he asked. "The bits and bridles?"

"Most of 'em. Lady Rutland's mare hardly needs a snaffle," the groom continued. "She's a good sidesaddle mount, goes quietly on a loose rein, and minds her rider's seat, leg, and whip. Some fool put a high port curb on her bridle. T' girths has all been switched aboot, too, and we'll be all day puttin' t' lot of it back to rights. Bad business, Doc Frenchie. Bad business indeed."

We left Carruthers muttering and cursing in the saddle room and met another long face in the barn aisle.

"The harnesses in the carriage house look right enow," the head lad said, "but what'll it be next? Turnin' the stud loose in the mare's pasture? Rutland is fanatical about all the foals not coming all at once-t and having a few dropped come autumn. He'll be proper turbulent about this mischief and sack somebody for sure."

"You should set out pickets," I suggested. "A night watch."

The man cast a look at St. Sevier, who declined to second my suggestion.

"We done that, milady, the first night after the sheep ended up in the garden. But as pickets has done since t' Flood, old MacArthur took a wee nap just after moonrise. He knew the horses would alert him to any strangers sneaking aboot the barn. I wouldn't know of MacArthur's lapse, except I came to relieve him and 'ad to wake him oop. I'd appreciate it if you'd not mention that to Rutland."

"We shall be discreet," St. Sevier said. "Back to work, Dunlap."

The old fellow shuffled off, head bent as if marching against a stiff wind.

To appearances, the barn had the peaceful air of a stable on a normal morning. The horses munched their first ration of hay for the day. An undergroom raked the dirt aisle near the barn door. Out in the yard, another undergroom scrubbed water buckets and refilled them at the trough.

But the grooms, usually a cheerful, whistling lot, were grim and braced for battle. The malaise affecting the household was spreading, and everybody knew it.

"I should change out of this habit," I said, moving off toward the stable yard, "and we must decide what, if anything, to say to Rutland."

"My lady, a moment," St. Sevier said, crouching. He studied the edge of the barn aisle, a spot the rake had missed. "A heel print only, but on the small side."

"Grooms who've worked with bloodstock tend to be diminutive." Racing jockeys were all fight and not much height, to quote my father.

"This lot is former military and Rutland keeps no bloodstock. Whoever made this heel print wasn't large." St. Sevier moved down the aisle a couple yards and pointed to another boot print immediately outside a stall door. "See how much more deeply that print sank into the dirt? A heavier person made it."

"Or one moving more quickly?"

St. Sevier rose. "Valid point, though moving quickly around horses is ill-advised."

I took his arm and leaned in close. "So is discussing this where we can be overheard." I pointed straight up, to the hay mow running the length of the barn above the stalls on both sides. A marmalade cat lounging on a crossbeam idly watched the swallows flitting about beneath the cupola.

St. Sevier escorted me out into the morning sun, and I felt a familiar mental energy take hold of me. We faced a puzzle, and I was not a magistrate or commanding officer, but I'd had some success solving similar puzzles and relished the challenge this one presented.

"We need to make lists," I said when we were out of earshot of the stable yard. "Who benefits? Who had the opportunity to pull these pranks?"

I braced myself for St. Sevier's usual protestations: We should leave, this is not our business, do not put yourself at risk of harm, my lady—I rather appreciated that one, though it frustrated me as well— except that St. Sevier was peering down the drive.

A big, dark gelding with an equally big, dark rider, hatless and graceful in the saddle, was cantering up to the Wood's front door. A vague recollection stirred as a groom trotted down the path to meet the new arrival at the mounting block.

"The cavalry has arrived," St. Sevier said, smiling slightly. "A bit behind schedule, as usual, but a welcome addition to the affray."

Before the rider had dismounted, I knew his identity: Sebastian MacHeath, Marquess of Dunkeld. "What on earth is he doing here?"

"You are not pleased to see your dear friend?"

Was St. Sevier teasing me or asking a serious question? "You and I left Scotland little more than a fortnight ago. I hadn't expected to see his lordship until next month, at the christening." I was pleased, of course, also a trifle... not pleased.

Parting from Sebastian had been difficult. He was a dear friend from my youth, but misunderstandings caused largely by my father's meddling had estranged Sebastian and me for years. Since I'd put off mourning, and Sebastian had taken up the search for a marchioness, he and I had become reacquainted.

The old ease we'd enjoyed was gone, but I still cared for him, and I hoped his feelings for me were again those of a friend. When I thought of my father cavalierly disregarding a very young Sebastian's request to court me and instead sending that heartbroken youth off to war... I was wroth with the earl all over again.

And lately, a little wroth with Sebastian. St. Sevier was attracted to me and desired me. He'd secured my permission to pay his addresses, and we were getting on at a great rate, though toward what end, I was not yet certain.

Why, all those years ago, hadn't Sebastian even once asked *me* how I would feel about a match between us? Why hadn't he dropped so much as a hint of his feelings to me?

"Why is he here?" I asked, changing direction to intercept Sebastian on the drive.

"Is his arrival a bad thing?" St. Sevier replied, ambling along at my side. "You said it yourself, they need an inspector general here. Somebody with a fresh eye and the rank to get some answers."

"Sebastian was Rutland's superior officer?"

"They both held the rank of colonel by the time they sold their commissions, but we are at peace now, despite somebody's best efforts to start a domestic war here at the Wood, and we are on British soil. A marquess, even a Scottish marquess, casts a mere baron into the shade."

Sebastian let his gelding walk the last fifty yards up the drive, though the horse would need more cooling out. The beast was sweaty, his coat matted with dust. The rider had clearly wasted no time on the journey south.

"You might have asked me, St. Sevier." He might have *warned* me was what I meant, though why should I need warning? "You might have run the idea of summoning the marquess past me."

"And if you had equivocated," he replied ever so pleasantly, "as women have been known to equivocate on even matters as important as whether to remarry? What then? Do you know how Wellington stopped the looting after his troops broke the siege at Badajoz? He set up a gallows and gave orders to flog any and all suspected miscreants. Rutland is ever one to admire Wellington."

"Rutland would make an example of somebody?"

"Turn MacArthur, Carruthers, or Bevins over to the assizes—possibly all three and a housemaid or two for good measure. That would mean weeks for some old soldiers and feckless women in one of your foul English jails, where jail fever or worse will likely kill them before the crown can order them transported, another sentence tantamount to death. The English are properly horrified at the excesses of French justice you refer to as the Terror, but in its way, English justice is all the more barbaric. You hang starving children for stealing a spoon."

He cited facts, drat him. "You will not distract me with politics now, St. Sevier. You should have told me you'd sent for rein-forcements."

"I was not certain he would come."

I strode forward to wait by the mounting block. "When his friends have need of him, Sebastian will always come, and you are most assuredly his friend."

St. Sevier sent me an impenetrably masculine look and waited quietly beside me. Sebastian swung off his gelding with the easy grace of the born horseman and patted the beast soundly on the neck.

"Put him at grass for a couple hours before nightfall," he said to the groom who took the reins. "No more grass than that, though he'll devour all the hay you can throw at him. Spring isn't as advanced up north, and we're still getting used to better rations."

"Aye, Colonel milord." The groom *saluted* before marching off with the horse in tow.

"St. Sevier." Sebastian nodded. "And my lady." A slight bow. "Monsieur tells me you have landed in the middle of another intrigue, Violet. Have you started making your lists yet?"

In my head, the list was growing by the hour. "My lists will have to wait. Your welcoming committee is about to descend."

Lord and Lady Rutland had emerged from the house and were making their way down the terrace steps. Tommie and Millicent MacNeil came behind them, and I rather expected we'd see the Joneses and O'Deas at luncheon.

Much smiling, bobbing, and bowing ensued, while St. Sevier waited patiently at my side.

"Well?" he asked at length.

"I have lists to make," I said, disentangling my arm from his.

"You are pleased to have Dunkeld's aid," St. Sevier said. "As am I."

St. Sevier was my lover, the man in whom I reposed as much confidence as I did any other human being, and he had done much to earn my esteem. He did not deserve my peevishness.

"Your instincts were right, St. Sevier. We need Dunkeld here if injustice is to be prevented. Will you meet me in my sitting room once I change out of this habit? We must decide what if anything to say, to whom if anybody, about the trouble in the stable."

He caught my hand and bowed quite properly. "I am yours to command."

He wasn't exactly, but then, I wasn't his to command either. Perhaps that had been his point in sending for Sebastian without telling me, to remind me of our uncommitted status.

I made my way around to the back of the house, where gardeners were at work replanting thinned lavender and moving irises that had yet to bloom. I wanted to question them, to ask who kept the keys to the garden gates, who had Bevins's responsibilities when he went to visit family.

I itched to make my lists.

I had itched to throw my arms around Sebastian in welcome, too, but I was not a hostess or relative to be permitted such a display, and he was not a soldier returned from war to deserve one. I was glad to see him, though.

Very glad, and not only for the sake of the old soldiers and feckless housemaids.

CHAPTER NINE

St. Sevier sent word by way of Lucy that he'd be unable to join me in my sitting room, as a council of war had been called in the library. I had not been invited, so it had fallen to me to browse the shelves up on the mezzanine—quietly—while the men mostly drank brandy and ranted on the floor below.

"I've a damned rebellion on my hands," Rutland said. "St. Sevier told me he'd sent for you, Dunkeld, and I wanted to throttle him. Even my guests thwart my authority."

"You see before you a contrite guest," St. Sevier replied as glass stoppers clinked against crystal decanters. "I sought only to aid my former comrades by summoning a disinterested investigator."

"A bloody marquess," MacNeil said. "Bit of a change from riding dispatch and waltzing at the regimental ball."

"MacHeath did a bit more than waltz," Jones muttered. "*Lord Dunkeld*, rather. I, for one, am glad you are here, Dunkeld. The ladies are growing concerned."

"What do we know?" Sebastian asked the question Rutland, or anybody with authority and sense, should have been asking.

Silence, and I had all I could do not to holler down at them to take up pencil and paper, create an order of events and a list of people who had opportunity to wreak each instance of mischief. That list should be followed by possible motives for each suspect.

"It started last year," Patrick O'Dea said eventually. "Little mishaps that you shrug off as an example of the grit life invariably kicks into your face. The first time I questioned whether we were dealing with more than coincidence was at the holiday open house. Athen—Lady Rutland goes all out, puts on quite a do, but the candles in the ballroom's chandeliers were tallow rather than beeswax. The stench was noticeable over the scent of pine boughs."

"An economy?" Jones asked.

Tommie MacNeil's distinctive heavy stride crossed the room. "That is not an economy her ladyship would permit. O'Dea is right. For the holiday open house, it's parade dress, spit and polish. We might have to resort to tallow candles this year, but I can say with authority that tallow was either a mistake or a deliberate attempt to tarnish the Wood's presentation."

"Has anybody spoken with the chandler?" Sebastian asked.

Another silence.

I heard a drawer opening and chair scraping. "I'll start there," Sebastian said. "What next?"

Finally, somebody was making a list, and I was curious to note that Rutland mostly allowed his subordinates to carry the conversation. By the time the first luncheon gong sounded, the men had described a dozen petty nuisances going back to before the Yuletide holidays.

They had not included the dented piano or the scorched curtains on their list, while the ladies' recitations hadn't included the tallow candles, parlor windows left open on winter nights, or a batch of ale going off. Truly, these people needed to acquire the fine art of talking to one another.

Perhaps they were too busy cavorting in conservatories and stairwells to bother with meaningful discussion.

"I will recruit Lady Violet and St. Sevier to aid me," Sebastian said as the gathering broke up. "Women will speak more easily with another woman, and St. Sevier is regarded with universal affection by the enlisted men. He's also adept at coaxing confidences from the unsuspecting, and his medical eye sees what others might miss."

"You will want to talk to the wives," Jones said. "They hear things too."

Imagine that. Women had functional ears.

"I will, of course, have a wee chat with the distaff," Sebastian said, "or ask Lady Violet to do so, but if I am to sit down to luncheon with the ladies, I had best make the close acquaintance of soap and water before the meal. Rutland, with your permission, I will also retrieve a book from this most impressive collection?"

"Help yourself," Rutland said as the voices of the others faded into the corridor. "I was furious with St. Sevier for summoning you, Dunkeld, and I'm still not best pleased by his insubordination. He was a volunteer, though, and they were ever prone to breaking ranks. He is also—damn him—right. We are in a muddle, and I have little clue how to resolve it."

"Not a criminal muddle, exactly," Sebastian replied. "But the situation is worrisome."

"I'm inclined to make a few examples," Rutland replied. "Sack a few footmen, let the head dairymaid go. Athena sets great store by her dessert recipes, and a ruined batch of cream..."

Of all the harms Rutland might have seized upon, it had not occurred to me that foiling her ladyship's ambitions for the dessert menus numbered among them. What sort of husband could both notice such a thing about his wife and so ardently disport with the woman who appeared to be his wife's best friend?

"If you sack the wrong people, you make the problem worse," Sebastian said. "You allow the guilty to go free, while giving them further opportunity to wreak havoc. Answers are reassuring, Rutland, but the right answers are the only ones worth having."

"You sound like Wellington." Oddly enough, this was not a compliment.

"His Grace relied heavily on his intelligence officers. I suggest you do likewise."

Rutland's footsteps moved toward the door. "I'll give you a week, Dunkeld. Free rein, provided you try to be somewhat discreet and don't upset the ladies. After that, as magistrate, I will invoke the king's justice as I see fit. This has gone on long enough."

The library door closed, while I pondered what it said about Rutland's character that he'd appoint himself judge and jury when he was himself a victim of the people he sought to arrest. That made him a vigilante, didn't it? A petty despot.

I did not care for petty despots *at all*.

"Violet Marie Belmaine," Sebastian called out when he was alone in the room below. "Get down here this instant and speak your piece. You keep me from soap, water, and twenty minutes on an obliging mattress at your peril."

I peered over the railing to see Sebastian, hands on hips, glowering back at me.

"My piece can wait until another time," I said. "Keep your assignation with the washbasin, my lord, and I will see you at luncheon."

I sashayed out the door that led directly from the mezzanine to the floor my apartment was on. So intent was I on making my grand exit that I collided with Lord Rutland and would have overbalanced had he not caught me in his arms.

"Upjohn took his supper plate to the table where I sat with the lady's maids," Lucy said, starting to undo the hooks of my evening gown. "Walters looked like Vicar had farted in church. I understand that somebody has to sit below the salt, but the tables are round, for pity's sake."

"What happened?" I asked. Upjohn was a former enlisted infantryman who now served as Sebastian's valet. They'd met the previous year in London under somewhat peculiar circumstances.

I liked Upjohn. He had joined the marquess's household with the humble good cheer of a foot soldier and had remained loyal to Dunkeld ever since.

"If you're the gentleman's gentleman to a marquess," Lucy said, "you sit where you please. When Upjohn finished eating, he got up to greet a pair of fellows he knew back in Spain, and that caused more scandalized looks. We cannot leave this place soon enough to suit me, my lady."

I had worn my gray silk evening gown down to supper, a subdued ensemble left over from half mourning. The other ladies, by contrast, had buffed themselves to a high shine, trotting out jewels heretofore unseen and elaborate coiffures such any Mayfair hostess might wear. Other than sending me a few brooding looks, Lord Rutland had given no sign he'd all but found me eavesdropping in the library.

I slipped the gown off and passed it to Lucy. "Do you have the sense visitors are a rarity here at the Wood, Lucy?"

"Rare as unicorns." She laid the gown on the bed and untied my laces. "You and Monsieur are the first since some old brigadier came through last summer with the hillwalkers. Seems a shame for so much house to go to waste. You heard about the problem in the stables?"

"I did, though I gather nobody has said anything to Lord Rutland about it."

"The staff was hoping the mischief would stop when visitors arrived, but it's instead getting worse. Let's undo your hair, my lady. If you're hiking up to the lookout again tomorrow, you'll want your rest."

The ladies had organized a picnic for the following day, about which I could muster little enthusiasm. I wanted to be interviewing footmen and questioning maids.

"If you can discreetly do so," I said, "please inquire about the nature of the incidents that have occurred previous to our arrival, Lucy. My sense is more is afoot than any one person knows, even Lord Rutland."

"His lordship is a *busy* man." Lucy gave the word a particularly disrespectful emphasis as she began tugging pins from my hair. "He hasn't so much as looked at me, and he had better not."

"You have my permission to geld him if he makes improper advances. The same goes for any man purporting to be a gentleman and acting like swine."

"What about the ones who aren't gentlemen?"

"The very same prescription. I take it you glimpsed his lordship and Mrs. O'Dea flirting?"

Lucy put a pile of pins on the vanity. "She's the buxom Irishwoman?"

"Mrs. O'Dea is stately and Irish."

The tugging resumed. "'Tweren't her. Was the little Welsh-woman, the dainty one, and such flirting as they were about can result in children."

Good heavens. I half expected any lord of the manor to take liber-ties with willing females, but I wasn't as accustomed to ladies so happy to oblige them. "Where was this?"

"The linen closet down the corridor. I wanted some sachets for your bedposts, and the underhousekeeper—the second underhouse-keeper, one of the Mary Whites—told me where to look. There are three Mary Whites on staff, you see. The door was half open, and the lady was sprawled upon a cedar chest, skirts up to her waist. His lord-ship were plowing atwixt the hills and valleys of Wales, so to speak."

Gracious God.

"He's a handsome man," Lucy went on blithely, "but this is his wife's house too. Struck me as unhandsome behavior. Why not lock the door, for pity's sake? Oh, the Quality."

The list I was making in my head was a list of couples, and it was growing long, tawdry, and complicated.

"The odd thing is," Lucy added, unbraiding the largest plait that had formed my cornet, "I had the sense he cares for her. He was loverlike, not merely rutting. She held his hand, laced her fingers with his."

I thought of how Rutland had tenderly caressed Kathleen

O'Dea's breast and her equally gentle explorations of his lordship's privities. The memory was shocking and intimate, but not vulgarly so. Whatever else was true, Rutland and Kathleen had feelings for each other.

And apparently, his lordship had feelings for Daphne Jones, too, and for his lady wife. Would Millicent feel neglected did she know of Rutland's tendency to stray?

"You will say nothing of what you saw, Lucy. We aren't here to stir gossip."

"How can there be gossip when nobody talks even at table?" Lucy retorted. "Did you know there are also two Jenny Smiths on staff here? Both chambermaids. I haven't met them, but then, I'd hardly know it if I had. I'm that glad to see Mr. Upjohn, I am. He isn't too high in the instep and never will be."

Mr. Upjohn's exact dealings with Lucy fell under the *none of my business* heading. "Lord Dunkeld has come to help sort out the Wood's troubles. I ask you to keep your eyes and ears open, Lucy, because staff will not talk openly to titled visitors in the normal course."

"Eyes and ears open, mouth shut. I know the drill, but it's not as if anybody has anything to say here besides 'pass the salt' and 'spring is coming right along.'"

Lucy finished with my hair, her brisk dispatch at variance with St. Sevier's soothing touch. I knew the men might make a long night of it in the game room, likely regaling Sebastian with the same war stories St. Sevier had heard not a week past. When Lucy had finished tidying up—and dawdling—I took up a shawl, donned house slippers, and made my way down the darkened balcony to St. Sevier's sitting room.

I had no sooner settled onto the sofa with a pamphlet about sheep husbandry in the north of England when the door clicked open,

and both Sebastian and St. Sevier—arguing, predictably
—joined me.

"We won't learn anything from that lot," Sebastian said, stopping
short just inside the door. "They closed ranks years ago. I see you
have company, St. Sevier."

Hugh affected affronted impatience. "I asked Violet to meet us
here, Dunkeld. There is no other place on this estate where we can
be guaranteed privacy. The staff is vast and always bustling about,
and MacNeil, O'Dea, and even Jones are frequently underfoot."

Sebastian eyed me on the sofa, curled up in my velvet dressing
down and shawl. I was more than decently covered, but the situation
was still horrendously improper. I resisted the urge to tuck my skirts
more closely over my feet.

"Did you bring your list?" I asked Sebastian.

Ever practical, he allowed me to preempt further discussion of
the proprieties. "I did. Somebody wants to make life at the Wood
difficult." He took a wing chair opposite the sofa, as did St. Sevier.

"But why?" St. Sevier asked. "Why pull these nasty, sly tricks?
The whole staff is made to look incompetent, and thus Rutland and
his subordinates are made sport of as well."

"Let's start with what we know," I said. "The trouble began last
year, with somebody swapping out the tallow candles for the beeswax
at the Christmas open house."

St. Sevier and Sebastian exchanged an *I told you so* look that
probably related to the coincidence of my searching for a book on the
mezzanine that morning while the menfolk blustered and swilled
brandy in the library.

"I spoke to the village chandler this afternoon," Sebastian said,
and how I had missed even the sound of his lovely burr. "He is a
former gunnery sergeant who believes in organization and schedules.
Her ladyship put in the order for the beeswax candles, which are
made from the Wood's own hives. He filled the order, boxed up the
candles, and they were duly carted up to the hall by a pair of porters."

"Do we talk to the porters?" I asked.

Both Sebastian and St. Sevier were still in evening attire, and I had to admit, they'd made a fine sight escorting the ladies into supper. Sebastian, as the highest-ranking male, had accompanied Lady Rutland, while Lord Rutland had been at my side. We'd been a handsome company, and the two handsomest men were now closeted with me and trying to solve a puzzle.

I took a moment to savor the fact that I was *happy*. I loved unknotting an intrigue, I was increasingly smitten with Hugh St. Sevier, and I had missed Sebastian. To think of him so far from Town, where I dwelled, had been a heartache, even though I knew he was devoted to his Scottish estates.

"I spoke with the porters," Sebastian said. "They carried the boxes of tapers to the usual pantry and left them there. Cleaning the chandeliers and affixing the candles is the footmen's job, and I will take up the narrative with them tomorrow."

"What of the confusion in the saddle room this morning?" St. Sevier asked. "That could have resulted in injury or worse."

I had had the same thought. If Lady Rutland's mare had been loaned to me for an outing, and a groom unfamiliar with the horse had inadvertently kitted out my mount with a harsh bit, I might well have come to grief. Being unfamiliar with the horse, I would have had no ability to sort high spirits or contrariness on the mare's part from genuine distress.

"That had to have been the work of somebody regularly in the stables," Sebastian said. "MacArthur fell asleep, I know, but the horses and cats would have alerted him to a stranger prowling around the barn. Whoever slipped into the saddle room was a known quantity and took the time to tie up the gear in exactly the manner in which they'd found it, the better to hide their tracks."

"St. Sevier suspects it might have been a woman," I said when Hugh declined to offer that opinion himself. "We found a diminutive heel print, though a groom had already raked most of the barn aisle."

Sebastian wrinkled a splendid beak. "Was the print small enough to belong to the groom on duty?"

I deferred to Hugh's recollection.

"*Non.* He was stout."

We got down to the business of putting incidents in order—a good dozen, so far—and kept bumping into the same conclusion: The Wood was being attacked from within. Too much intimate knowledge of the household was involved with each mishap.

Somebody had known, for example, exactly how the dairymaids spent their days. They rose earlier than the rest of the household to milk the cows before breakfast, and thus their nooning was a midmorning meal. They frequently napped in the afternoon before tending to the evening milking.

Somebody had known that pattern and thus been able to sour the cream without fear of detection.

Somebody had known when the family parlor would stand empty and a porcelain figurine could be knocked to the hearthstones.

Somebody had known when the footmen cleaning the paintings would take a tea break so minor damage could be done to the brigadier's portrait without anybody the wiser.

"The staff is enormous," I said, "easily twice what my father employs at Derwent Hall. The men are largely former military, the women local. They all need their jobs, and they all know the Wood is struggling financially."

"How do *you* know that?" Sebastian asked. "The grounds are impressive, the house more so. The horseflesh is first rate and in good weight, the sheep wintered handily, and the staff looks reasonably well fed. There's not a pothole in the drive or a sagging portion of the stone walls, and the house is spotless. How do you *know* the finances are troubled?"

"Mutton and potatoes," I said. "Lucy claims the fare for most of the staff is worse than pedestrian. An orange on Sunday is a great treat."

Sebastian looked unimpressed. "Before the kitchen gardens come in, plain fare in springtime isn't unusual."

"Not that plain, not with walled gardens, winter gardens, and a conservatory the size of Green Park."

"What of the village?" St. Sevier asked, likely to head off a good bicker between Sebastian and me. "Is it as well maintained as the manor?"

Sebastian turned over the piece of paper on which he'd made his list of incidents and scribbled something.

"No, but I attributed a few loose chimney bricks and papered-over windows to the usual toll winter takes. The church is tidy, though I understand services are held only once a month."

"Suggesting," I said, "that somebody is reluctant to pay for the living, and curates from nearby take turns on the first Sunday only. Another economy."

"Do we look at unhappy younger sons?" St. Sevier asked. "You English set great store by your rights of succession. Perhaps Rutland was to have died in battle so that a cousin might inherit?"

"And this cousin is trying to wreck the place by a thousand cuts?" I mused. "When he eventually murders Rutland, he comes into possession of an ailing estate pushed—by the self-same heir—to the brink of ruin. *We English* aren't generally that stupid."

"That's up for debate," Sebastian said, sounding very Scottish. "Who is Rutland's heir, and how much of the estate is entailed?"

"Add it to your list," I said, covering a yawn behind my hand. "There's something else you should know."

Another look passed between the two men.

"I told him," St. Sevier said. "Our host is quite frisky." He made the admission exaggeratedly French. *Our 'ost ees quat free-skee.*

"Not only our host," I muttered. "I learned tonight that Rutland's paramours include both Daphne Jones and Kathleen O'Dea, though his lordship also seems genuinely devoted to his wife."

"His lordship lighted Mrs. MacNeil up to her apartment after you left the parlor tonight," Sebastian said. "He was some time rejoining the company, and nobody remarked it."

St. Sevier peered into the flames on the hearth. "Does such vigor leave one admiring or appalled? Perhaps Rutland has a French grandfather."

"Our host isn't the only vigorous member of the assemblage," I said. "Patrick O'Dea is disporting with Mrs. MacNeil, and Daphne Jones accosted St. Sevier *en plein air*."

Sebastian also took to considering the fire. "As I walked back from the village, I spotted Garth Jones and Lady Rutland in the gazebo by the stream. Their embrace was..."

"Passionate?" I suggested. "What is going *on* with these people? They live in each other's pockets and have to know vows are being slighted."

"Vows," St. Sevier said, "are being enthusiastically disregarded on every hand. The French are rational enough to distinguish between spousal loyalty and marital fidelity. Perhaps the English are learning a similar sophistication? These men love their wives, and clearly, the wives esteem their husbands. May I suggest that marital frolics are not relevant to the reason Dunkeld has joined the gathering?"

I turned a glower on St. Sevier. "In my lexicon, loyalty to one's spouse implies fidelity, sir."

St. Sevier smiled at me pleasantly. "In mine as well, which is why Mrs. Jones's attempts to charm me from the path of gentlemanly decorum were unavailing. Might we return to the matter at hand?"

"Please," Sebastian said. "I have Upjohn making inquiries among the footmen and gardeners, some of whom he knew in Spain. I trust the fair Miss Hewitt has been recruited to the cause?"

Another bicker averted, this time between St. Sevier and me. Why must gentlemen be so disobliging?

"Lucy says matters belowstairs are in a most peculiar state. Mealtimes are segregated by rank and gender, conversation is limited and stilted, and visitors to the manor are a significant rarity."

Sebastian turned his gaze on me. "Why is a rarity of visitors this far north significant?"

"Because we are in the middle of the hillwalkers' paradise, Dunkeld. For those unwilling to travel on to Scotland, the

Lakes are as close to heaven as anybody in search of beautiful scenery will come. The traffic increases year by year, and the hotels and boardinghouses are all reserved far in advance. With as many military connections as Rutland has, some of those old friends would doubtless be inspired to visit him in high summer."

Sebastian scowled, a thoughtful sort of scowl. "The grouse hunting is good hereabouts as well, and given the terrain, fox hunting is a foregone conclusion. You are right: Visitors in the person of old military friends should plague the Wood without number. A house party or two would be quite well received."

"If those old friends are as randy as Rutland and his subordinates," I observed, "a house party would soon devolve into an orgy." I had given up on a mental list of who frolicked with whom, for apparently, ladies and gentlemen at the Wood paired off with whomever they found in the vicinity of a handy stairwell, linen closet, or conservatory.

"While the staff barely speak to one another," St. Sevier murmured. "I find that troubling, particularly when staff has been let go without provocation. That always causes talk and is further proof that the Wood's revenue is inadequate to meet its expenses."

"Rutland has been sacking the slackers?" Sebastian asked, adding another note to his paper.

"Not slackers," I replied. "Female staff only and without any deficiencies in performance to justify his actions. The terms of separation are generous, but it's always the women turned off. MacNeil argues that former soldiers are owed more loyalty than local girls and women who have family and friends in the area. Then too, he claims that footmen can be made to dust and scrub, while a maid cannot lift furniture."

Society doubtless agreed with MacNeil, while I took a dim view of his reasoning. Footmen could dust and scrub, but would they? And maids did move furniture, something MacNeil would know if he'd ever seen them at work.

"If I were a maid," St. Sevier said, "and I wanted to tip the balance away from more women losing their jobs..."

"You'd make the men look bad," Sebastian said. "Utterly logical, because a man who'd ruin a family portrait or tamper with bridles deserves the sack."

"And if I were the male staff," I said, "and I did not want to be unjustly accused of mischief I did not commit, I'd shatter the nearest porcelain shepherdess and sour a batch of cream while it chilled in the dairymaid's domain."

"Rutland has provoked a domestic war," Sebastian said, "but we still have to identify the ringleaders or the hostilities will have no end."

"Or," I said, "they will end in tragedy."

CHAPTER TEN

"I will light you back to your room," Sebastian said, rising and extending a hand to me. "The hour grows late, and we must consider our theory for what motivates Rutland's troubles."

St. Sevier's expression remained perfectly genial as he also got to his feet. "This theory has the ring of truth. It explains much."

I stood, surprised at how tired I was. "You say that because the idea occurred to you first, though I must admit, skirmishing gangs of domestics makes sense. Moving an entire flock of sheep without waking the household doubtless took coordinated effort."

"As did swapping out entire boxes of tapers," St. Sevier said. "A determined woman is not to be trifled with, and an army of determined women should give any man pause."

Sebastian took a carrying candle from the mantel, used a spill to light it, and held the door for me. "I will make it a point to speak individually with Rutland's subordinates tomorrow on our picnic outing. St. Sevier, if you would speak with the ladies?"

"*Bien sûr.*"

"What does that leave for me to do?" I asked.

"Enjoy the scenery?" Sebastian suggested.

"I'll speak with Rutland. He's a puzzle, and for a man of infamous tirades, he's grown very quiet."

"Excellent point," St. Sevier said, bowing over my hand. "Until breakfast, my lady."

Did he mean that? Was I to leave him in peace to ponder his theory in solitude?

"Come along." Sebastian winged his arm. "I am weary beyond belief, and the corridor grows chilly."

We walked arm in arm the short distance to my sitting room door. I opened it and realized I hadn't lit any candles.

"I will do the honors," Sebastian said, using his candle to light a branch on my mantel. "Was there a reason why you could not trust me or St. Sevier to convey to you the developments in the library today, Violet?"

"So glad to see you too," I replied, standing before the hearth and holding my hands out to the flames. Now that Sebastian had mentioned the chill, I felt it.

"Violet, you must promise to tread lightly. These are military men, they know their way around firearms, and you appear to have stumbled into a nest of unhappy marriages sitting atop a few score unhappy domestics."

"These marriages don't seem unhappy, my lord. They simply seem *porous* or flexible. Everybody has a jolly time with the nearest available partner, then we meet for civilized meals while the staff commits mayhem between silent, spare suppers."

Sebastian braced an arm on the mantel, his posture weary. By the flickering firelight, he looked piratical and nearly grim.

"Rutland has given me one week, Violet. You heard him, and to be honest, a week is about all I have to spare."

Sebastian was fastidious to a fault, and in adulthood he'd taken to wearing a scent that was mostly cedar with hints of sandalwood. I closed my eyes and inhaled through my nose, trying to parse the middle notes of what had to be a personal fragrance.

"What is your hurry?" I asked. "Must you retreat to the High-lands to toss logs about by the midsummer moon?"

"Cabers, ya wee besom. We toss the caber, and dance, and down a few drams between rounds of tug-of-war. I've business to attend to in London. Clemmie dunned me into going south a few weeks early rather than waiting until we christen your new nephew."

Clemmie being Lady Clementine, Sebastian's only sibling. "You are back to hunting for a marchioness?"

"Clemmie says I must, and I do not argue with my sister, particu-larly when the aunties forbid me to."

Sebastian's Aunt Maighread and Aunt Hibernia were the epitome of formidable dames. "What of your daughter?" A sprite of about seven whom I had not met. She had returned with Sebastian when he'd come home from the war, and I knew two things about her: She had been born outside of wedlock, and Sebastian loved her dearly.

"She will visit Clemmie until I return north. I am to write to her every Monday without fail and mind my penmanship when I do."

Sebastian was a marquess, enormously wealthy, and a handsome man in his prime. He would be swarmed with marchionesses-in-waiting the instant the matchmakers learned he was in London. They would overlook his tendency to height and brawn and even—so gracious of them—overlook his Scottish burr and the fact that his family seat was in Perthshire.

"Shall I make you a list?" I asked when what I wanted to tell him was to go home and enjoy springtime in Scotland.

"Of women suited to become my wife?"

"Of the ones to avoid. Some of those ladies have gambling prob-lems, others are too fond of the poppy, still others have sisters nobody has seen for years, supposedly visiting relatives in Wales."

"I'll manage," Sebastian said.

A silence bloomed, and I realized Sebastian hadn't touched me since arriving at the Wood. Hadn't bowed over my hand, hugged me, or bussed my cheek. In Scotland, he'd been affectionate and somehow more relaxed. At the Wood, he was the inspector general I'd requested and more the stranger I'd met in London a year ago.

"I'm glad you're here." I spoke as Sebastian murmured, "I'll bid you good night."

"It's late," he said. "The next week will be busy, and I suspect a handsome Frenchman waits up for you."

"A little waiting up won't hurt him. We are only courting, after all."

"St. Sevier asked me to come, Violet. That was no small concession to his pride, but he feared you would poke a hornet's nest, and he hasn't the standing with these people to intervene properly."

"He told me he sent for you, and I am glad you are here."

"Then I am glad to be here. Sweet dreams, besom." He brushed a kiss to my cheek, and I caught him in a hug.

"I worry about you, Sebastian MacHeath. I don't like to think of you racketing about that castle with only aging relatives and one small child for company, but I dislike the idea of the matchmakers having at you even more."

He hugged me back, a good, solid embrace, nothing careful or reluctant about it. Something incomplete inside me sighed and relaxed, and then Sebastian stepped back.

"I have been to war," he said. "A few quadrilles and a waltz or two won't be that difficult, and first we'll see to Rutland's difficulties."

"Then I wish you pleasant dreams."

He offered me a jaunty bow and slipped out the door, as silent as a breeze. I stood for a moment before the fire, trying to sort out my feelings and getting nowhere. Sebastian had come because he'd worried for me, and maybe for St. Sevier, the perpetual outsider who'd inadvertently come upon a war in progress.

St. Sevier, who had said he'd see me at breakfast, the wretch. If he wanted to spend the night alone, he could tell me that to my face, and I would leave him in peace. I banked the fire and opened the French doors only to find Hugh standing on my balcony, his expression anything but welcoming.

"You will not go off alone with him," St. Sevier said, taking me by the hand and pulling me in the direction of his sitting room. "You will not be heedless with propriety where anyone can remark your lapses. Just because we find ourselves in the middle of an English bacchanal does not mean you will risk your—"

I wrenched free. "You are *lecturing* me?"

"I know you," he said with soft emphasis. "I know you, and may the good God help me, I love you. I do not trust that man, and neither should you."

I marched into his sitting room, ready to offer him a few pointed corrections about whose behavior was trustworthy and whose behavior was the outside of too much. St. Sevier followed me, his gait that of a stalking lion.

"If you think," I began, "for one instant, that you can tell me what to do, St. Sevier, or with whom to do it, then you are very much mistaken. Egregiously mistaken." *We are not married*, I wanted to add. We weren't even engaged, and perhaps we never would be.

The vehemence of my reaction startled me, given that I had been alone with Sebastian late at night and passingly affectionate with him, while St. Sevier had apparently spied on us. St. Sevier's behavior was unbecoming of a gentleman, while mine...

I still yearned for a return to the easy trust and taken-for-granted friendship I'd had with Sebastian years ago, but I had to reconcile myself to the fact that life had moved on for both of us. He was to take a marchioness, and I was contemplating marriage to St. Sevier.

Or I had been.

He prowled up to me. "If you think, Violet Belmaine, that you can nip off into the woods with Lord Rutland, there to coax confidences from him at peril to your safety, while I charm the ladies with my *delightful accent*, you are hideously mistaken. More mistaken than Bonaparte's fleet taking on Nelson at Trafalgar."

My mind stumbled twice. Firstly, because St. Sevier had said he loved me—*in English*. Secondly, because we were arguing at cross-purposes.

And what a relief that realization brought. I smoothed his hair back from his brow. "Nelson died at Trafalgar."

"A hero's death, and you are not to indulge in similar risks, Violet. Rutland clearly takes what he wants from the women at the Wood, and they have little choice but to yield it."

"That bothers me," I said, closing the French doors and crossing into the bedroom. "Are they willing or not?"

"He holds their husbands' livelihoods in his hands," St. Sevier said, following me. "How can the ladies feel free to refuse Rutland when he's the lord of this petty fiefdom?" He tugged at his cravat, his movements brusque.

"Let me do that." I brushed his hands away and undid the knot. "Lucy saw him in flagrante delicto with Daphne Jones. They looked like lovers to her, tender and intimate, not merely pleasure seeking."

St. Sevier glowered down at me. "Now you are opposed to pleasure?"

My lion was either glowering for form's sake or teasing me. I kissed him, a leisurely plundering of his lovely mouth, then drew off his neckcloth and started on the buttons of his waistcoat.

"Shared pleasure is all well and good," I said, "and I think you are forgetting that Lady Rutland is making free with the husbands."

"Again, do they feel free to refuse her overtures? I am not sure they do."

"And Millicent and Patrick on the stairwell? Daphne Jones importuning you?"

"Patrick O'Dea is simply behaving true to form. I treated him twice for the bachelor's complaint in Spain, though I suspect with him the affliction was somewhat chronic. Illnesses without number were chronic in the camp, and our establishment was healthier than many others."

"The bachelor's complaint?"

"The Covent Garden ague, the Drury Lane flu. It ran rampant

in all its several forms, closely followed by everything from measles to dysentery to chicken pox to mumps. Quartan fever wasn't unheard of, and some variety of jail fever often afflicted the infantrymen. The consumptive gravitated to the artillery—less marching—and habitual drunkenness was most common in the cavalry."

"And here I thought the battles were the worst war had to offer. Shirt off."

St. Sevier pulled his shirt over his head and handed it to me. The garment was an extravagant affair of softest cotton, the tucks where the arm and shoulder joined too numerous to count. Lace adorned the wrists, and the buttonholes looked to have been finished with satin thread.

He sat on the arm of the reading chair angled before the hearth, a casually beautiful, half-naked, complicated man.

"On Bonaparte's retreat from Moscow," Hugh said, "fever killed more men than the Russians did, and the Russian army is notoriously good at killing. I lost a brother on that grand exercise in arrogance. Felled by a swift bullet, thank the merciful God."

I stepped between his legs and hugged him. "I'm sorry." Sorry he'd lost brothers—three of them, truth be told—sorry a man with a healing vocation had begun his medical career facing death on every hand.

He allowed me to hold him, the moment imbued with intimacy of a sort that had nothing to do with bacchanals. *I love you too.* The words resonated in my heart, though the moment was not right to speak them.

"Wash up," I said, stepping back and filling the warmer with coals. "And I will take care where Rutland is concerned. I doubt he likes me very much, and I am certainly not among his admirers."

St. Sevier disappeared behind the privacy screen. "A man need not like a woman to find her attractive."

I flipped back the blankets and ran the warmer over pillows and sheets alike. I had leaped to the conclusion that St. Sevier wanted to dictate to me where Sebastian was concerned, when in fact Hugh had been expressing a need for caution regarding Rutland.

"Is Rutland capable of rape?" I asked, not liking to even speak the word aloud.

St. Sevier emerged from behind the privacy screen, his falls half undone, his hair damp. "Under the wrong circumstances, we are all capable of abominations. You would kill to protect those you loved, Violet, and so would I, I hope."

What would Rutland do to protect those he cared for? What had he done?

"Did you ever treat him for the bachelor's complaint?"

St. Sevier peeled out of his breeches and draped them over the vanity stool. "I cannot recall, nor would I reveal such a personal aspect of his medical history to you if I did recollect it. I treated half the camp for half the known afflictions of mankind. I also delivered many fat, healthy babies. Into bed with us, please."

We made love without preliminaries or flourishes, a comforting reestablishment of closeness that banished the day's frustrations to a manageable distance. St. Sevier fell asleep almost immediately thereafter, and I should have followed him into slumber.

Instead, I remained awake, watching shadows dance on the ceiling, my arms wrapped around a man who had seen too much and cared for too many. Compared to St. Sevier, my husband had been a shallow, selfish boy, and the difference between them gave me pause. Had I been a shallow, selfish girl? Was I more than that now?

I curled closer to St. Sevier, watching his muscular chest rise and fall in slumber. So many evils could have taken him from me, bullets not the least among them.

"*Je t'adore.*" I whispered the words to him in his native tongue, hoping they found their way into his dreams. He was truly lost to the arms of Morpheus, else I should not have offered him the rest of it. "*Je t'aime.*"

For I did love him, very much.

~

"This is the current list." Tommie MacNeil passed me three pages of foolscap. "You'll please not lose it, or my Milly will be most displeased."

Each name was tidily noted, surname first. "This is the whole female staff?"

"Should be," he said, opening another drawer in the estate desk. "Inside and outside, village and manor, divided up by job. That's Milly's system, and I question it at my peril. The male staff is simply alphabetical, with each fellow's job noted beside his name. I've another list of pensioners, if you've a mind to interrogate them too?"

"Interview, Mr. MacNeil, not interrogate."

He came around the desk and passed me another list. "I understand why the staff is upset. Rutland doesn't grasp that we're not in Spain anymore. He can't just go issuing orders and expect them to be followed without question."

The male staff list was longer than the female list, and both included more than two score names. "You think the whole staff is upset, or are we dealing with a few agitators?"

He propped a hip on the desk and scrubbed a hand over his face. "Doesn't really make any difference, does it? When you talk to the ladies, you'll find none of them know anything. The dullest recruit soon learns that if you peach on your mates, you might as well be drummed out of the corps. When French bullets are flying, you might live to regret your honesty, or you might not. Milly would agree with me, and she knows the female staff far better than I do."

Was that a warning? It certainly wasn't small talk. The great picnic expedition was soon to depart for the lookout, but I had these moments to interview MacNeil.

"When did Mrs. MacNeil become your assistant?"

"Call Milly that, and she will be quite blunt with ye, my lady. Milly merely helps out with a few details, to hear her tell it, but I'd be lost without her, and I don't mind tellin' ye that. 'Twas the same in

Spain. The quartermaster has to be everywhere at once, and nobody is ever glad to see him unless he's driving a wagon of supplies. Milly kept a sharp eye out and spoke up for the laundresses and cooks and other ladies when the officers expected them to wash clothes without soap and stitch up uniforms without thread."

His gaze was on memories I could not see, but the esteem he expressed toward his wife sounded genuine.

"I will copy these lists and return them to you," I said. "Where would you start if you were questioning the maids, Mr. MacNeil?"

"Call me Tommie. Everybody does." He pushed away from the desk and cracked a window, letting in an eddy of fresh spring air. "I'd send St. Sevier to have a wee chat with the housekeeper about the medicinal stores. That man could charm a stone saint into confiding in him. All the ladies were happy to discuss their complaints with Doc Frenchie, and for good reason. He took care of us. Went toe to toe with Rutland on occasion when it was needed. Wish he hadn't turned MacHeath loose on us, though."

I pretended to study a painting of a chaotic battle, the usual expiring and semi-dismembered infantry and horses in the foreground, a gallant officer mounted in the middle of the mayhem, colors waving behind him in the gun smoke.

"You don't care for Lord Dunkeld?" I asked.

"He's a good man."

True, of course. "But?"

"But now that he's on hand, we cannot pretend we've simply been plagued by wee mishaps. Rutland will insist on an example being made, probably several examples, and exercising that kind of authority is bad for morale. Milly has held her peace so far, but she sees how hard the womenfolk work, and forced marches and short rations are desperate measures, not how an army thrives."

MacNeil had learned some diplomacy in his post as quartermaster. "You're saying it's wrong to sack the staff?"

He brushed a fingertip along his mustache. "Not wrong, foolish. The estate needs a certain number of hands to be kept up. If Rutland won't reduce his holdings—and legally, that would be difficult—then reducing staff beyond a certain point means we fall behind. If we're short-handed, we cannot shear the sheep as quickly to get the benefit of early-market prices, so our revenue falls.

"We don't do as thorough a job with the apple harvest," he went on, "so we have a smaller crop. We have to use our shepherds to assist the dikers to repair the stone walls, and foot rot gets started in a herd some inexperienced lad has been left to tend. Next thing ye know, a once-pretty estate is a ruin, and nobody wants to work here."

"What is the solution?"

He smiled, a merry and self-deprecating expression. "A wee dram now and then." He produced a silver flask from a breast pocket and offered it to me.

"No, thank you."

He tipped the flask to his lips, capped it, and slipped it back into his pocket. "Rutland is a good man, and I need to see the Wood thrive as badly as anybody does. There's nothing for me and Milly back in Ayrshire, and she has friends here. I walk a delicate line with Rutland as a result. We all do. I hope you'll recall that, as you and MacHeath go poking your noses into cupboards that should remain locked."

"Would Rutland make an example of one of his subordinates?" I disliked that idea. However unorthodox the intimate goings-on at the Wood, this was a family of sorts. Singling out one of the three trusted minions as an example could only create great ill will.

MacNeil's gaze went to the gory painting. "If an example is to be effective, it should be shocking enough to make a strong impression, shouldn't it? I once thought I could predict his lordship's behavior, but I can no longer make that claim." He moved toward the door. "Be careful, Lady Violet. If you can do so without causing offense, tell St. Sevier and MacHeath they need to be careful too."

He sketched a bow and withdrew, leaving me with much to consider.

CHAPTER ELEVEN

"I could not find the third Mary White or the second Jenny Smith," I said as Sebastian took a seat on the railing around the gazebo. "The other two Mary Whites—in fact, all the maids—were reticent to a fault."

St. Sevier lounged in the gazebo's doorway, gaze on the stream burbling along several yards away. The spot was peaceful and secluded, as good a location to compare notes as to tryst.

I had pleaded digestive unrest and quietly explained to my hostess that the female indisposition had befallen me. Thus had I avoided another hike to the lookout, leaving Sebastian and St. Sevier to make the best of that excursion without me.

I would have to speak with Lord Rutland another time, but speak with him, I would. If he turned on his own associates and made an example of a subordinate, a couple who had followed Rutland through many vicissitudes would be unjustly punished.

Unless, of course... one of the couples was behind all the trouble?

"You've had a thought," St. Sevier said. "Out with it." He had been notably silent since returning from the picnic, though he had heeded the suggestion to chat up the housekeeper about her herbal.

"What if the mischief is not a war between maids and footmen, but between, say, Patrick O'Dea and Tommie MacNeil?"

"Or O'Dea and Rutland?" Sebastian said. "You think this is about all the dodging into linen closets and fondling in the conservatory?"

"Passion and jealousy have inspired many a crime." I had certainly harbored dreams of retaliation for Freddie's many infidelities, though my retaliation would have been against Freddie only, not the ladies who took his proffered coin.

St. Sevier ambled away from the door to take a seat beside me on one of the padded benches. "But who is the wronged party in such a situation? The first to stray? The first to proposition? The spouse who was indifferent or gruff one too many times such that straying grew appealing? We will never sort that out."

Hugh was in a pensive mood, suggesting something had occurred in the course of the day's hike. Something he did not find cheering. Daphne Jones again?

"We might sort it out," Sebastian said. "Rutland is the superior officer, and he's making free with everybody else's wives. No matter how willing the ladies might be, or appear to be, the husbands could take exception."

"So the husband's take exception by importuning Lady Rutland," I replied. "The score evens."

"Or," St. Sevier said, taking up a fallen acorn and pitching it into the water, "the fair Athena is evening the score, and our contest is between the lord and lady of the manor. Just as the ladies would be reluctant to refuse Rutland, the gentlemen would be in an awkward position if importuned by her ladyship."

Hugh had mentioned this notion once before, that a woman could intimidate favors from men not strictly eager to indulge her.

"Tell us about the maids," Sebastian said. "Who is the third Mary White?"

I put aside speculation about marital-revenge motives with some relief, for the topic struck a little too close to home. Freddie's family had looked askance at me immediately following his passing, though the coroner had found nothing suspicious about Freddie's death.

My in-laws and I were still merely polite to one another. I had done nothing to mend the breach, nor did I plan to.

"The staff is so large," I began, "and surnames in the locality so limited, that several of the women have the same name. There are two Jenny Smiths—I spoke to one—and three Mary Whites. I met with two of those, and they resemble each other somewhat. I also noted two Elizabeth Barrows and two Charlotte Clearys. The men's list has two Thomas Postlethwaites and two David Farradays."

"We had the same problem in the army," Sebastian said. "You'd yell for Private Taylor to fetch your horse, and three men would march off to the paddock."

I shifted on the cushion, which was more decorative than functional. "The housekeeper said the maids are occasionally sent into the village on errands. I will find the errant ladies, but I fear it's as Tommie MacNeil predicted: They've closed ranks against intruders."

I rose, needing to pace. My womb ached, as was sometimes the case when my menses befell me. Walking usually helped, but this stroll down to the gazebo had not. I was frustrated and out of sorts as a result of a wasted day chatting up the maids and undercooks, and my physical woes would probably worsen before they improved.

"The housekeeper was similarly reticent," St. Sevier said, pitching another acorn. "She chattered on about the staff enjoying good health generally, and she was happy enough to show me her herbal stores, but she had nothing to offer regarding any loose sheep or misplaced candles."

"Candles are within a housekeeper's purview, usually," I said. "The butler gets the remains of unfinished wine bottles, the housekeeper gets the candle-ends to melt down and sell. On an estate like this, there's probably a thriving barter economy belowstairs, with footmen dicing for beer rations and maids using weekly allotments of candles and tea as stand-ins for coin."

"Also like the army," St. Sevier said, "where rum, flour, and tobacco became forms of currency."

"Tell me about your hike to the lookout," I said, because discussion of habits belowstairs wasn't likely to gain us much.

"So scenic," St. Sevier said, waving a hand. "Beautiful, lovely, invigorating. Such fresh air, such fine sheep, such stately pines. I found a moment to confer with Mrs. O'Dea, whose husband is genuinely considering a remove to Ireland. Patrick sees no path for advancement here, he misses his homeland, and Kathleen said he is lonely and bored."

That Kathleen would pronounce her husband lonely and bored struck me as insightful.

"Paddy O'Dea is gregarious," Sebastian said. "He was good for morale in Spain. Flirted with everybody, always had a joke and song for the men, got along with the generals and privates alike. A Cumbrian backwater is no place for the likes of him."

And yet, he'd bided here for several years already. "Did Mrs. O'Dea have anything to say about the sheep in the garden and so forth?"

"She said she wished she'd thought of it." Sebastian seemed unhappy with that response. "Said it was the sort of prank to liven things up without doing any harm, and Rutland needed to ease up on the reins."

I paced a small circle in the gazebo, my heels creating a slow tattoo on the floorboards. "What of the other ladies?"

"Lady Rutland is worried," St. Sevier said. "She worries for her husband, but she also worries for the others. They are nearly all the society she has, and she knows matters are growing difficult."

"And Mrs. MacNeil?"

"She and Tommie have talked of emigrating," Sebastian said. "Cutting ties and starting anew before they get too old and lose their nerve. They both have family in America, and the letters from the cousins report much opportunity for those willing to work hard."

"They both work hard," I muttered as St. Sevier handed me a

half-dozen acorns. I pitched them, one by one, into the water, making a bull's-eye of the center of the concentric rings my first throw had caused. "The Wood is on the verge of falling apart. Who benefits from its ruin?"

"I asked Lady Rutland who the heir is," Sebastian said. "She named a cousin, also in America, born and bred there, and with no interest in returning to Cumbria."

St. Sevier passed me more acorns. "So much for that theory."

So much for all of our theories so far. "This is how a puzzle is unraveled, gentlemen. The confusion mounts as we gather more information, and then, if we persist, we stumble across one fact or turn of phrase that illuminates the whole. We are just getting started, after all."

"We have seven days," Sebastian said, "and one of them is more than half gone. You will likely spend the rest of it in bed swilling chamomile tea, unless I miss my guess."

I glanced at him sharply, but he was affecting the bland expression a mischievous Scotsman adopted so well. "How can you tell?"

"Here." He tapped the center of his forehead. "You don't frown, but you betray a tension, and you are pacing slowly."

St. Sevier watched this exchange with his own version of an unreadable expression. He was my intimate and a physician, also capable of counting to twenty-eight, and yet, I was more embarrassed that Hugh would hear this discussion, than that Sebastian would accurately guess at my bodily woes.

"As a younger woman," I said, by way of explanation, "I was vociferous about the injustices of biology toward women. Lord Dunkeld heard more than a few of my tirades."

"You were merciless," Sebastian replied mildly. "You terrified even your oldest brother, who was insufferably dignified from a young age."

I had. Mitchell's ears turned red when I spoke of a woman's monthly miseries. I'd forgotten that.

"The herbal," St. Sevier said, smiling slightly, "is well stocked with chamomile and the usual remedies favored by females. Chamomile with ginger and cinnamon might ease your complaint, my lady. You will find them on the shelf above the fennel, chasteberry, and raspberry leaf."

The one shelf eased menstrual complaints. I wasn't sure what the other shelf was for. "What malady do those herbs cure?"

"They can be used as tonics for the womb," he said gently. "Treatments, not cures, for some conditions relating to conception. Fennel is also quite effective for treating the wind and an excess of spirits. Raspberry leaf can ease loose bowels or infections of the lungs."

I was sorry I'd asked. "Back to your outing." I resumed pacing. "What had Mrs. Jones to add to the discussion?"

St. Sevier was all out of acorns. He sat directly across from Sebastian, crossed his arms, and cocked his head. "My lord Dunkeld, you have the floor, as the English say."

"Mrs. Jones was eager to show me the vista to the north."

"She dragged him off into the bushes." St. Sevier smiled evilly and had turned *booshez* into a synonym for an alpine seraglio. "Our little Scottish lamb went all unsuspecting to a terrible fate."

Sebastian looked bored. "She was friendly."

"She was wound around him like the ribbons on one of your English maypoles. Her overtures to me were tame by comparison."

"Jealous?" Sebastian retorted.

I stood between them, feeling equal parts affection and exasperation. "Kiss and cuddle with whomever you please, Dunkeld. Heaven knows everybody else at the Wood adopts that attitude, but did Mrs. Jones say anything that pointed toward the Wood's problems?"

Sebastian gazed out over the quiet stream, and my, he made a handsome picture. Whereas St. Sevier was all elegance and lean grace, Sebastian would become craggy in old age. Both men were formidable, and both dear in different ways.

Whoever Sebastian's marchioness was, she'd be a lucky, lucky woman.

"Mrs. Jones," he said, "claims her husband is going to waste here, that a man of his talents should be running multiple businesses, not serving as a glorified secretary to a rural martinet."

Daphne Jones had held hands with that martinet when making love with him in a linen closet.

"She struck me as desperate rather than passionate," Sebastian added, "and no, Violet, I do not find desperation much of an aphrodisiac. Besides, it was chilly up there."

I smacked his shoulder, though I had no idea what the temperature of the air had to do with obliging Mrs. Jones's desperation. "Don't be rude."

"Exactly," St. Sevier said. "She has in some regard tossed caution to the wind. Why? What purpose does leaping upon a handsome and charming Frenchman, or backward, homely Scot, serve?"

"Or upon Rutland?" I added.

Sebastian rose. "This backward, homely Scot is off to begin interviews in the stable, seeing as the latest problem originated there. St. Sevier, my lady." He paused in the doorway and speared St. Sevier with a look.

"We will walk slowly back to the manor," St. Sevier said. "I will order my lady the tisanes and fetch her a rousing novel or some French poetry, as she wishes. I will join you in the stables only when that mission is accomplished."

"I am not a mission."

"Safeguarding your wellbeing," Sebastian said, "had best be St. Sevier's highest duty and sacred privilege, or he will be one backward, bruised French charmer. Good day to you both."

He ambled down the steps and struck off along the path that wound along by the river.

"I don't know what to say to that." I did not know what to *feel* about that behavior, half protective, half arrogant.

"You say thank you," St. Sevier replied. "To your Scottish bear and to me. Dunkeld and I are both aware that this puzzle you long to unravel could soon grow dangerous, so you will take my arm, and we will totter back to the manor like the harmless older couple I pray we someday become."

I took St. Sevier's arm, but I could not quite manage to totter, not even for him.

~

St. Sevier made me up a concoction of chamomile tea and warm spices. The taste was different in a pleasant way. The result was an easing of my miseries. That he would know of such recipes and prepare one for me was a reminder that my favorite Frenchman had, at one time at least, been passionate about his medical calling.

Most physicians left women's discomforts to the herbalist or consigned them to the realm of fancies intended to seek attention. It occurred to me, not for the first time, that if Hugh St. Sevier had been my physician, I might not have lost two babies.

A baby now would be a tremendous complication, one I was not prepared to cope with, so my courses brought a sense of emotional relief even as they discommoded me physically. Hugh was scrupulously careful to take measures to avoid conception, but none of those measures was foolproof.

"Shall I fetch you a book?" he asked when I was comfortably ensconced in my sitting room with a tray of his magic tea. "Or will you pore over your lists?"

"I might do some embroidery. My mind works while my hands are busy." This was true, though I had no intention of doing needlework.

"I will find Dunkeld, then." St. Sevier leaned down to kiss my cheek, though I caught his hand and prevented him from moving away.

"You should resume practicing medicine."

He sank onto the sofa beside me, our hands joined. "That would be easier were I in Scotland or France. The English... Their medicine is considered quite hopeless by the rest of Europe."

"Because we distinguish between surgeons, apothecaries, and physicians?"

"In part. Your physicians question, they do not examine. Your surgeons take little heed of standards of cleanliness that date back to the guidance of Paracelsus. Your apothecaries care more for patent remedies than the proper uses of herbs. You thwart anatomical studies with medieval church laws, and thus your science does not progress."

"Are you choosing between me and medicine, St. Sevier?" I had not considered moving to France or Scotland, but neither would I reject those options out of hand—assuming St. Sevier and I eventually married.

"*Non.* You encourage my vocation."

I cuddled closer. "I feel better. Not one hundred percent, mind you, but less uncomfortable." And he had probably prepared this brew for the ladies of Rutland's camp, assuming the ingredients had been available. No wonder they all loved him.

He obliged me with an arm around my shoulders. "Shall I stay with you?"

"You want to be out in the stable poking hornet's nests with our favorite Scot." Who was neither backward nor homely.

"What I want..." St. Sevier sighed, and I did believe the French were better at sighing than the English would ever be.

"What do you want?"

He kissed my cheek and spoke very quietly. "To belong to you."

That brave declaration made my heart beat harder. "Why?"

"Because you encourage me where other Englishwomen would be scandalized by how I want to practice medicine. Because you poke hornet's nests and inspire me to do likewise when I would instead hide away with my pamphlets and treatises. Because you have earned the loyalty of the marquess who does not impress easily, and the respect of your mostly heedless and self-absorbed family." He kissed me again, this time on the temple. "You did not allow the melancholia to steal your fire."

"*You* did not allow the melancholia to steal my fire." He'd suggested, teased, gently scolded, and ultimately challenged me to leave my malaise behind, and for that alone, I would always love him. Hugh St. Sevier, without any drama or heavy-handedness, had saved my sanity, if not my life.

"You are so very dear," I said. "I wish I were not indisposed."

"Your indisposition does not preclude intimacies, Violet. In fact, an interlude can do a better job of banishing the female ache than my tisanes, which I'm told are quite effective. Conception is also most unlikely when you are bleeding."

I sat up. "You enjoy shocking me. You look all polite and concerned, though you are earthy too. I treasure this about you, but I also know you are dying to see what Dunkeld has got up to, so be off with you."

"I am banished," he said, rising. He paused to cup my cheek against his palm and treat me to a kiss the likes of which would ensure I missed him thoroughly. "I go to my humble duty and will prevent my lord Dunkeld from blundering into the arms of more lonely wives. So thankless, my duty, but I am inured to such hardships."

"I will want a report before supper," I said, patting his falls as he straightened. "Don't think to avoid me, because I will put Lucy up to interrogating Upjohn, and all will be revealed."

He pressed my hand over inchoate evidence of male enthusiasm for procreative activities. "You torment me. Until supper."

I let him go and refused to gratify his nonsense by sighing aloud, though it was a very near thing. Perhaps the air at the Wood made consenting adults frisky, perhaps I was, to use my brothers' phrase, arse over ears in love.

I gave St. Sevier ten minutes to return on some pretext, then finished my tisane and took another look at my lists. The third Mary White was a senior chambermaid, and thus her duties included making the beds in the footmen's dormitory.

That struck me as a strange division of labor, but such was the strength of tradition in great houses that the practice probably arose in centuries past. At Derwent Hall, where I had been raised, we used boys rather than scullery maids to scrub pots. The boot-boy typically graduated to that duty and from thence to underfootman.

In other homes, no male help of any sort was permitted in the kitchen. In still others, the entire kitchen fell under the supervision of a chef.

The footmen's dormitory was located on the third floor, while maids typically slept belowstairs. This arrangement was intended to foster propriety, though I suspected it fostered a great deal of mischief on the servants' stairs instead.

I folded my list of staff into a pocket and made my way to the next floor above. The windows were smaller and farther apart, the air close, the quiet oppressive. Were I a footman, I'd remain downstairs in the warmth and bustle of the kitchen and servants' hall as late as possible before seeking a cold bed in the house's upper reaches.

I was impressed again, though, with the sheer size of the Wood. A house party on such an estate could comfortably welcome dozens of guests as well as their footmen, maids, grooms, and coachies. I opened a door at random and found a spare, clean bedroom on the other side. More doors led to similar quarters suitable for senior staff, companions, or visiting tradesmen.

Farther down the corridor, I found a nursery suite, complete with two rocking horses—one for Lord Rutland, one for his deceased older brother?—and a pall-mall set neatly gathering dust in a corner. Had the boys played pall-mall on the rug? The playroom alone had to be twenty feet on each side and the schoolroom almost as commodious.

I closed the door on the nursery, finding the space disturbing. Somebody dusted up here, somebody occasionally aired the rooms and had the rugs beaten. Still, I would learn nothing relevant by handling forgotten toys and browsing old storybooks.

I made a thorough inspection of the entire floor, including two footmen's dormitories, probably senior and junior. Both were as neat as barracks on the day of inspection, with the beds made up, an extra blanket folded across the bottom. Beside each bed was a night table holding a candlestick, an empty glass, and *A Book of Common Prayer*. Some night tables held a second book, and a desk in the corner displayed writing implements.

I had seen worse accommodations for domestics, but I had also seen better. One hearth heated the entire room in both dormitories. The only chair was at the writing desk, and the walls were bare. Not a single rug provided protection from floors that had to be frigid in winter, and no sachets leavened the faint stench of coal smoke permeating the air.

I cracked a window and treated myself to a bird's-eye panorama of the garden and the pine-covered hillside beyond. At least the footmen had a gorgeous view. I hoped they had the time to enjoy it as well. I left the window open a few inches and made my way back down the corridor. I had found no Mary White making up the beds and no answers either.

I paused to once again peer into the nursery, and a queer sensation prickled over my skin.

The couples at the Wood were all relatively young. I'd guess the ladies were not yet thirty, and the men weren't much their senior.

As enthusiastically as they all seemed to cavort with one another, and as long as they'd been married, where were the children? Where on earth were the children?

"I should have seen this sooner," I said, plucking at the tassels of a pillow fringe. "Not once have any of the ladies referred to offspring with that half-proud, half-burdened air mothers have. No one has referred to sorting out squabbles among staff in the nursery. The ladies do not date the major events in their lives from when this or that infant was teething. The lack of children is glaring, once noticed."

"No ponies in the stable," St. Sevier murmured from the other reading chair.

"No stray toys left on the lawn," Sebastian added, dumping some coal on my sitting room hearth and poking air into the fire. "You are right that a lack of children is peculiar, but perhaps these people don't want children, given the..." He waved a hand.

"Ongoing orgy?" I replied. "No means of avoiding conception is entirely effective, and the couples at the Wood seem enthusiastic about their pleasures." Before I'd left the upper floor, I'd taken a moment to enjoy the view of the lake from what might have been a governess's parlor. I had seen Tommie MacNeil and Kathleen O'Dea disappear into the summer kitchen—a building not yet in seasonal use.

His hand had rested on the small of her back, and she had made no effort to evade his touch. None at all.

"So we add another piece that might belong to this puzzle," I said, tossing the pillow aside. "No children." A piece that disturbed me. "I am the logical party to investigate this aspect of life at the Wood."

"You are," Sebastian said, replacing the fire screen. "We met both Lady Rutland and Mrs. MacNeil in the stables, visiting their mares."

"Were they?" St. Sevier asked, leaning his head back to stare at the ceiling. "When I am in the mood to commune with my trusted mount, I bring him an offering. An apple, a carrot, a few extra strokes with the soft brush, ten minutes at grass. The ladies brought no such treats."

Sebastian turned to brace his shoulders against the mantel, hands in his pockets. "They were spying on us?"

"Supervising us, perhaps. With their presence, reminding the grooms to keep mum, which they did."

"Rutland doesn't want you here, Dunkeld," I observed, "which suggests to me he knows more than he's telling."

"They all do," St. Sevier muttered. "I can smell the secrets as plain as manure, and yet, there Rutland sits, lord of all he surveys, allowing his household to fall into disarray. He doesn't have all the answers, not if he's allowing that to happen. A failure of command is his worst fear."

"Agreed," Sebastian said. "I have the sense he truly loves this estate and has done all in his power to preserve it."

"And yet," I said, rising, "he has no heir of the body. That has to be part of what's afoot here."

St. Sevier sent me a disgruntled look. "What can a lack of babies possibly have to do with sheep in the garden or candles put in the wrong boxes?"

"I don't know," I said, "but we are getting closer to the solution if Lady Rutland and Mrs. MacNeil are watching your every step. I'm off to find Rutland."

St. Sevier and Sebastian exchanged a look.

"I know," I said, "be careful. The closer we come to answers, the more upset somebody is likely to be with us. I will venture no farther than the estate office, where his lordship is likely to be at this time of day. I know this because the housekeeper has orders not to allow any servants to interrupt him when he's at his ledgers. I gather the accounting is a source of woe for his lordship. Perhaps he'll welcome a distraction."

"You've had an idea," St. Sevier said, rising and regarding me with the sort of expression that suggested I was being diagnosed. "I will not like this idea."

"I will hate it," Sebastian added. "But neither St. Sevier nor I are foolish enough to try to talk you out of it. We will expect to see you whole and healthy at supper, my lady."

Did he know what I had planned? I suspected he did, and he wasn't stopping me. I had a theory about the cavalier disregard for marital vows at the Wood. I was determined to test my theory.

I found Lord Rutland at his desk, his characteristic gentlemanly turn out compromised to the extent that he'd shed his coat and turned back his cuffs, the better to deal with ink and sand.

"My lady." He rose and began rolling down his cuffs, his expression pained rather than welcoming. "I hope nothing urgent compels you to intrude upon me when I'm at such a humble task."

"That depends." I closed the door and locked it, which his lordship noted with a raised eyebrow.

I came around his desk and took his coat from the back of his chair, holding it out to him. A gentleman would never be caught in company without his coat, but I had ambushed Rutland in his masculine sanctum sanctorum, and he and I were not children.

I eased the coat up his arms and smoothed the fabric over broad shoulders. He was as well made as his coat, even if he did lack the inches to be truly imposing.

"I am all ears, my lady," his lordship said, taking a sleeve button from the blotter.

"Allow me." I held out my hand. He treated me to a moment's scrutiny, then passed me the sleeve button. I affixed it to his shirt cuff, then did up the second cuff. In doing so, I brushed my fingers over his wrist, a passing caress that Rutland did not appear to notice.

"Firstly, my thanks for your hospitality," I said. "Shall we sit, my lord?"

He gestured to the sofa, and I assumed the seat in the middle. Rather than take a place on either side of me, he perched a hip on the corner of his desk.

"I did not relish an immediate return to London," I said, "and when St. Sevier suggested this detour, I was more than happy to tarry at the Wood."

"I trust our hospitality has been above reproach?"

His higher vantage point would have allowed him to leer down my bodice, which I had tugged as low as modest fashion allowed before embarking on this interview. Not very low, in truth, but I still felt somewhat exposed without a shawl.

"Your hospitality has been gracious."

"We don't have many visitors at the Wood, and I know Lady Rutland looked forward to the prospect of seeing St. Sevier again. He was a favorite with the womenfolk and quite competent medically."

His lordship, in other words, had not looked forward to the prospect of seeing St. Sevier again—nor had anybody been particularly excited to make my acquaintance—but Rutland had concluded that refusing to host a visit would have been rude.

"Did St. Sevier ever have occasion to treat you, my lord?"

"In passing. I was in the throes of a bout of smallpox when he arrived. For a time, I feared I would face the ignominy of death on a damned cot in the surgery rather than on the battlefield. St. Sevier credited a strong constitution with my eventual recovery."

And good medical care had had nothing to do with it, of course. "You were never inoculated?"

"My brother was sickly, and my mother was convinced inoculation would serve him ill. St. Sevier had the whole camp inoculated, over many objections, but I saw the wisdom of it."

"St. Sevier is quite determined in his way." *Persistent too.* "I am here on his behalf in a sense, though he would doubtless prefer I hold my peace."

Rutland cocked his head, his expression half amused, half resigned. "Then why don't you?"

"Because a lady's good name is involved."

"Not yours, I trust?"

"Are you teasing me, my lord?"

He shook his head. "Tending to the ledgers is the bane of my existence, Lady Violet. The totals are invariably too large under some columns and too small under others. Not even for the delightful prospect of bantering with you would I put off my daily penance with the abacus."

He was dutiful, in other words, and I liked that about him. Respected it. I set aside that inconvenient conclusion and forged ahead. "Mrs. Jones has been indiscreet."

"And how is this any business of mine?"

I rose and went toe to toe with him, standing closer than a lady ought. "She was indiscreet with you, sir."

His gaze became very cool. "I will not dignify that accusation with a response."

"I did not expect you to, but she has also made advances to St. Sevier—you witnessed them at the same time I did—and just yesterday, she threw herself at Lord Dunkeld. This is the sort of situation that provokes duels and tragedies, and I am not in a position to intervene."

"Thank God for small mercies." He sidled away from me and scrubbed a hand over his face. "Dunkeld mentioned this to you?"

"I overheard St. Sevier teasing him about it." A version of the truth. "Neither man will take what was on offer, but if somebody doesn't learn some discretion, I fear for the consequences."

"You can't help yourself, can you?" He sent me a speculative look. "You must put right what you see as wrong. You call it an instinct for justice. Others call you a meddler."

"You are not offering me a compliment, my lord." Still, his insight took me aback. I hadn't taken him for a stupid man, but neither had I accorded him much intuitive intelligence.

"I am commiserating, my lady. I was known in the army for being a stickler for military protocol, but I contend that I was a stickler for rules that had been created for good reasons. Enforcing those rules prevented small problems from becoming larger problems, though others would argue the point. When I saw the rules disrespected, I knew greater folly would soon follow, and all too often, I was right."

An interesting speech, and not relevant that I could see. "Then observe the rules of common sense when disporting with Mrs. Jones, sir. Close and lock the door to any linen closet, for example."

He winced. "I concede nothing, but your point is noted. Might I return to my ledgers, my lady?"

Rather than leave him as requested, I once again stood immediately before him. "You will speak to Mrs. Jones?"

"When the moment is right, and I will thank you to leave the discussion entirely in my hands. Life at the Wood can be lonely for the ladies, and they manage as best they can. Mrs. Jones would not appreciate being confronted with your accusations."

Were the men lonely too? Was all this adultery caused by a want of quarterly assemblies?

"I will keep my peace, my lord, though silence can create more problems than it solves, like those broken rules you so abhor."

He peered down at me, the same half-amused, half-pained look in his eyes. "I like you, Lady Violet, more than I want to. Nonetheless, you and your pet mastiffs will never ferret out the cause of the Wood's problems if you waste your time peering through keyholes at passing frolics that are none of your affair."

I smoothed my hand over his lapel, an exceptionally presuming gesture. "I don't have to peer through keyholes when the closet door is half open, or when couples disport in stairwells, *in the conservatory*, in the gazebo, and on the way to the summer kitchen. You have all become so casual about your *frolics* that you forget to exercise caution. I suspect you have stopped seeing what's right under your noses in other regards, and for that reason, St. Sevier, Dunkeld, and I will get to the bottom of your troubles."

He stepped back. "To deduce who scratched a portrait of the brigadier, you need not pass judgment on the peccadilloes you think you observe among the Wood's residents. I am warning you, Lady Violet, as much as it would pain me to be ungracious to a guest, you either ignore our little lapses at the Wood, or I will send you packing."

"I ignored my own husband's repeated little lapses, my lord. I grasp the concept of discretion, but I suspect the slashed portrait and the multitude of little lapses are related."

"Thank you for airing that baseless opinion," his lordship countered, unlocking the door. "My staff is in revolt, and your focus should be on determining why and whom to hold accountable."

I paused before him, because a point needed to be made. "And if the responsible parties are among your immediate subordinates? You have given Garth Jones, *among others*, an excellent reason to sabotage the Wood."

"It's not what you think, my lady." He said the words that participants in illicit trysts had been saying since the invention of linen closets. "Now, if you will excuse me?"

I treated him to a steady perusal. "The Wood is in trouble, my lord. Serious trouble, else you would have concluded this interview by ordering me to depart at first light. I truly do want to be of aid, and you truly do need my help."

"Then help," he said, opening the door and bowing, "but do not meddle."

I left with my head held high, though the interview had solved little. I had all but flaunted what wares I had at Rutland, and he'd not so much as glanced at my cleavage. He was a gentleman, apparently, despite my earlier sense that he might have been more than flirting with me. He was more enthusiastic about spending time with the dreaded ledgers than he was about either ogling my bosom or assisting me to solve the estate's problems.

Though solve them, I would.

CHAPTER TWELVE

For four days, Sebastian, St. Sevier, and I annoyed one another with pointless speculation, attempted to interview the staff, took walks all over the grounds, and generally got nowhere. I felt like a mouse, running in increasingly frantic circles while the cats looked on inscrutably and waited for me to exhaust myself.

We had two days before Sebastian had to travel on, and St. Sevier was making a case for observing our originally scheduled departure date as well, which would mean leaving the day after Sebastian.

"Our host does not want us to solve his difficulties," St. Sevier said, "and thus I suspect he has had a hand in the creation of them."

St. Sevier offered that conclusion as he and I idled on a swing that overlooked the stream, a private, quiet place where the progress of spring was beautifully in evidence. Somebody had had the great good sense to situate the swing on the edge of a bluebell wood that began at the water's edge. Between the early volunteers on the bank hinting at the wood's approaching glory, the peaceful burbling of the stream, and the particularly sweet sunlight characteristic of the region, I was enchanted.

Also disgruntled. I should have spent the past fortnight enjoying the area's immense natural beauty and the company of my escort, not chasing after elusive Mary Whites—I still hadn't caught up with Mary White the Third or Jenny Smith the Second—and avoiding the servants' stairs.

"What does Rutland have to gain by plaguing his own household?" I asked, because as outlandish as St. Sevier's theory was, it also intrigued me.

"His staff remains focused on keeping their jobs?"

"Why would they be focused on anything else? Stately homes kept up in the old style are fewer and fewer, and the staff here apparently prefer to work among former army comrades."

St. Sevier ranged an arm along the back of the swing. "The talk is that Bevins isn't returning. His sister found work for him in Liverpool, and he'll give up his place here rather than watch somebody be sacked who hasn't done anything to deserve it."

"How did you learn that?" I closed my eyes for the pleasure of feeling the warmth of the sunshine on my eyelids, and also because I loved simply listening to Hugh St. Sevier speak. That voice had eased a world of pointless anxieties when I'd been too overwrought to leave a house of mourning, despite wanting to badly.

"Dunkeld stood the company to a few pints down in the village. MacArthur and Carruthers got to talking with him over a hand of cards, and the innuendos were strewn among the empty tankards. He conveyed his findings to me over the port last night."

"Innuendos only. These people are extremely concerned for their posts." And I was concerned for the staff. Many of the men had served on the Peninsula, and the womenfolk had sent husbands, sons, and brothers to the military. They deserved better than constant upheaval and short rations. "The staff simply hasn't a motive for sabotaging the estate or preying on one another."

"Except they do have motive, because sooner or later, unless the price of wool rises, somebody else will be sacked."

"We're reasoning in circles. You had best kiss me."

Lips softly brushed my cheek. "Perhaps you ought to be kissing me, my lady. I have missed you lately."

The past week had been a revelation to me in at least one regard. I had assumed that because of my indisposition, St. Sevier and I would sleep separately. I had been in that drifting phase of slumber several nights past when he'd lifted me from my bed, carried me the length of the balcony, and deposited me in his.

The last thing I recalled from that night was St. Sevier muttering something about *ta place est avec moi.* Your place is with me.

Freddie had maintained a discreet distance from me at such times, and I had been content to have my privacy. I was more than content to have the comfort of St. Sevier's hands kneading the small of my back or his warmth wrapped around me.

Another reason to dread a return to London: I would no longer have my nights with St. Sevier, even the relatively non-erotic nights, and keeping that sort of company with Hugh was a luscious pleasure.

"What else have you and Lord Dunkeld kept from me?" I expected more kisses, but I got a considering silence. I opened my eyes. "St. Sevier?"

"One of the lady's maids, Miss Walters, put a peculiar sequence of medical questions to me, professing to ask on behalf of her nephew."

"But because of your vast stores of professional discretion, you won't even hint about the nature of the conversation." I had run into St. Sevier's professional discretion before. The cliffs of Dover were mere hillocks in comparison.

St. Sevier's arm shifted to settle on my shoulders. "I do not believe she was asking on behalf of any nephew. She was curious about medical means of enhancing masculine vigor."

"She need only breathe the fine Cumbria air, from what I've observed. The Wood is awash in masculine vigor, and in feminine vigor as well."

"But not in babies, which is—"

Dunkeld came striding along the stream bank, and when I would have popped to my feet and smoothed my skirts, St. Sevier's arm gently prevented me.

"My lord, good day," I managed.

"Not a good day," Sebastian countered. "Damned Rutland is holding a drumhead court-martial on the back terrace and preparing to turn Carruthers over to the assizes."

I was off the swing in the next instant. "Hurry. Rutland will never change his mind once he's made a decision." Eyes front, forward march, and all that, though I did not march, I *ran*.

"My lord, a word, if you please." Sebastian spoke softly but with an implacable note of authority I would never have attributed to the contemplative friend of my youth. Gimlet blue eyes promised Rutland severe consequences if he thwarted Sebastian's request.

"You will not gainsay my authority in my own home, Dunkeld."

Sebastian cast a glance around the terrace. Two burly fellows, probably porters based on their garb, stood on either side of the stalwart Carruthers. Old MacArthur was also present, as was the lad I'd seen raking the barn aisle the morning after all the girths and bits had been disarranged. Patrick O'Dea, Garth Jones, and Tommie MacNeil formed a row at attention, and another person—the stable master?—stood a few paces off, looking quietly thunderous.

"I do not seek to gainsay anybody's authority," Sebastian said, "but this is not the place for a summary proceeding. Half your domestics will observe from the windows."

"Let them," Rutland snapped. "This nonsense has gone on long enough, and I have identified the culprit. The more public the example, the better."

"Then present your evidence," Sebastian said, which simple command had the effect of deposing Rutland as judge and jury and putting him instead in the prosecutorial role.

"Green." Rutland waved an imperious hand. "Tell them what you told me."

The young stable lad shuffled forward. "I wasn't tryin' to eavesdrop, milord, but I did hear ye." The boy was near tears, cap in hand, unable to meet MacArthur's gaze.

"Say on, Green," Sebastian said. "We're simply having a civil discussion and trying to get to the truth."

Rutland inhaled through his nose so pointedly, the windows ought to have shaken. He was genuinely upset, also genuinely in his element, hurling accusations and prepared to hurl thunderbolts as well.

"Down at the Pint and Pie," the boy said, "I heard MacArthur telling you Carruthers was the one to suggest we set a watch, but then Carruthers... Well, he wasn't very alert on his shift."

Rutland crossed his arms. "You heard MacArthur admitting that, but how do you know it personally, Green?"

"Because I got up in the middle of the night myself to..." He pointedly looked away from me. "Take some air, and I seen Carruthers catching a few winks. I figure he said to set a watch so he could switch all the bits and girths about without getting caught. Elsewise, he might have stayed awake to catch the culprit when he sniggled his way into the saddle room."

"I did see ya, ya daftie," Carruthers barked. "I figured ya wasn't planning on enjoying the moonlight all on yer lonesome."

The boy's face turned bright red, suggesting Carruthers had guessed correctly.

"Carruthers had the expertise and the opportunity to wreak dangerous havoc in the saddle room," Rutland said, dropping his arms and pacing before his subordinates. "He is discontent with his wages. Last autumn, he sought promotion to head lad, and I denied him that opportunity. Grant had more seniority."

"Not in the stable, he didn't," Carruthers retorted. "Grant's a good man to work for, meaning no disrespect, but he came to the

Wood nigh six months after I did. He were a corporal, though, back in the day, while I was just cannon fodder."

"Motive," Rutland said, pivoting smartly. "You can see Carruthers resents his lot. He had motive, means, and opportunity, and he's insubordinate when confronted. I say let the judges at the quarter sessions sort out the rest."

Sebastian watched Rutland pacing, while St. Sevier was studying the pretty garden. Not a one of the trio of minions had spoken so much as a word, nor did they seem inclined to intervene.

"My lord, you have no *proof*," I said, striding forward. "From what I can deduce, the riding horses enjoyed days of idleness before St. Sevier and I sought to go for a morning hack. Any groom on the premises, under the guise of cleaning the bridles and saddles, could have switched out a bit here, a girth there, and nobody would have been the wiser. Was Carruthers the only candidate for head lad besides Green?"

O'Dea spoke up. "Carruthers, Grant, Millbank, and Dandridge all expressed interest in the post, and I put Hammerschmidt forward as well, though he did not apply."

"And how long ago was this?" I asked.

MacNeil deigned to answer. "October."

"So we have at least two others with means, motive, and opportunity," I said, "if the intention was to make Mr. Grant look bad, because of a possible slight committed by you half a year ago. Do we send them to the assizes too?"

"*They* did not pretend to take watch and instead take a nap!" Rutland all but bellowed.

Little did his lordship know, bellowing menfolk had figured in my upbringing from a young age. Loud arguments everywhere from the stable to the dinner table to the game room to the coach on the way to Sunday services had inured me to the sound of a male in a pet.

"Have you *asked* Dandridge and Millbank if they took a shift on the night watch?" I countered.

"They did," Grant said. "We all did. Nobody wanted to see the problems at the house start at the stable. Foaling season is upon us, so we'd soon be setting night watches in any case."

"Well, my lord." I came to a halt about six paces from Rutland. "Do we round up the entire stable staff and commend them to the quarter sessions? Should we include Mr. Green's sweetheart, because she's likely to provide *him* an alibi? He's clearly a young man with an ambition to better his station so he might one day be able to marry. Discrediting Grant might serve his scheme quite well.

"Then too," I went on, "we can send the entire stable crew to the assizes, and that doesn't solve the riddle of who scratched the brigadier's portrait, because stable hands are unlikely to even know what painting I'm referring to. Did Carruthers switch out boxes of candles in the dark of night, despite having no notion where the candles are stored? Did he somehow gain access to a locked ballroom, all unnoticed by the liveried servants working there, or have the time and cunning to dent the piano? What a busy man Mr. Carruthers is."

O'Dea winced. MacNeil and Jones stared straight ahead. I had the odd sense both St. Sevier and Sebastian were trying to contain smiles, but I was not amused. To effect this drama, Rutland had to be growing desperate—not desperate to find answers, but desperate to stop the investigation from proceeding.

"Please focus on the issue at hand, my lady," Rutland retorted. "Serious harm could well have resulted from the mischief in the saddle room. A girth the wrong size, a harsh bit, a fractious or fresh mount—"

Soft footsteps pattered across the terrace. "My lord, I apologize for interrupting." Lady Rutland, looking more worried than apologetic, took the place to her husband's right. "What are we about here?"

Before my eyes, the imposing commanding officer became the doting husband. "We're sorting through a few possibilities," Rutland said. "No need for alarm, my dear."

Milly MacNeil and Kathleen O'Dea bore down on us from the

direction of the conservatory. Their approach occasioned an exchange of looks between the husbands.

"You are dismissed," Rutland said to his stable crew, "but do not leave the property until you have further orders."

They shuffled off, with Carruthers tossing a glower over his shoulder and MacArthur patting him on the back.

"You did this on purpose," I said, watching as Rutland murmured something in his lady's ear. She was smiling now, the worry gone as if it had never existed. "You put on a display, my lord, but why?"

"Because," Rutland said, "you lot haven't found any answers. I've thrown a proper scare into the enlisted ranks. They will either get to the bottom of the problem without further intervention from the officers, or the nonsense will stop of its own accord."

"I daresay you're right." Lady Rutland took her husband's arm, presenting an unmistakably united marital front. "It's one thing to twit a commanding officer or to engage in a bit of mischief to safeguard a post, but to send a comrade-in-arms to the assizes won't serve."

"My lord, you should have thought of it sooner," MacNeil said as his lady wife ascended the steps with Mrs. O'Dea. "A few lashes to a known malcontent will settle down the entire barracks."

"Not settle down," I said before O'Dea and Jones could offer Rutland further congratulations on his brilliance. "Intimidate, bully, abuse. This is not the army, and your little display will do nothing but further divide your staff and erode morale. You forget, my lord, your staff is not indentured to you for life. They can leave at will, just as you sack them at will."

Now St. Sevier winced, while Sebastian murmured a quiet, "My lady, have a care."

"You have more staff than you can afford," I said, marching up to Rutland and poking him in the chest. "Now, everybody from Mary White the Third to Thomas Postlethwaite the Younger will quietly seek other posts, and by summer, only sots and scalawags will care to work at the Wood. Problem solved. Well done, my lord."

I expected to provoke a tirade with my blunt speech, or at least a cold reprimand. Instead, Lord Rutland gazed at me almost pityingly.

"Clearly, my lady, the Wood's situation distresses you, and for that I am appreciative. Just as clearly, you can no longer find the repose and pleasure a guest on the premises ought to enjoy. Your coach as well as Dunkeld's will await you after breakfast tomorrow."

He bowed and withdrew, Lady Rutland on his arm. The other couples left without sparing me even a glance, leaving me with Sebastian and St. Sevier.

"*That* was his objective," Sebastian said. "To drum the three of us out of the regiment and to do it before witnesses who will say his decision was justified."

"We tried." St. Sevier's sigh did not strike me as half so elegant as usual. "We did try."

"Rutland steered me into the ambush of his making," I said, feeling both frustration and grudging admiration. "I obligingly charged straight into his trap. If I read him correctly, he has just protected his forces at the cost of his fortress. I will take a tray in my room for supper."

I left my loyal guard on the terrace, doubtless bemoaning my impulsive and outspoken nature, while I took myself down into the lovely spring garden. I had spoken to every member of the female staff save the third Mary White and second Jenny Smith.

The staff, to a woman, were unable to shed any light on the trouble that should have been laid at their slippered and booted feet, and yet, Rutland's first choice of culprit hadn't even been an inside servant, much less a female.

Truly, he was desperate to see me and my loyal guards sent upon my way.

~

"I borrowed this from the herbal," St. Sevier said, brandishing a curious object. "They have abundant stores of them and will not miss this one. I was opening drawers, looking for a pencil, and came upon quite a supply."

"What is it?" I asked, taking it from him. "This looks like a common sponge with a ribbon tied about it."

He ambled behind the privacy screen, leaving me at the vanity.

"That's all it is here in England," he said, "a sponge with a loop of ribbon securely affixed, but on the Continent, it's a popular means of contraception. It occurred to me that your education regarding such measures was less than extensive."

"How does one...?" The ribbon was a jaunty red and knotted tightly.

I heard water splash against porcelain.

"One soaks the sponge in vinegar or lemon juice and inserts it into the female orifice prior to coitus. The seed cannot as easily reach the womb and encounters the vinegar or lemon juice, so there is less chance of a baby."

My late husband had found it uproariously amusing to try to tempt me into sexual games and adventures, some of which I'd allowed him to try, most of which I'd found beyond ridiculous. My concern at the time had been *increasing* the chances of conception, though I well knew the reverse concern could also be pressing.

"And I am to use this?" I had to wait for an answer until a freshly scrubbed St. Sevier, naked from the waist up, emerged from his ablutions.

"I love children," he said, "but I will not use conception to trap you into speaking your vows with me, Violet. If you conceive, you will do so despite my attempts to prevent it."

I considered the sponge, a common enough household item, particularly in kitchens and sculleries. What woman had first taken the notion to soak it in vinegar and...?

"I am apparently willing to risk conception," I said, setting the sponge aside, "because the only certain means of preventing it is beyond me where you are concerned."

"I am irresistible, alas," St. Sevier said, peeling out of his breeches. "You are unlikely to conceive now, as your courses are ending, and for a few days thereafter. I show you the sponge as something to consider, though I am happy to demonstrate the specifics of its use at your request."

The sponge was scratchy-soft in its dry state. "It doesn't hurt?"

"Ideally, the vinegar or lemon juice is warmed, but no, there is no discomfort for either party. You use the ribbon to remove the sponge after the lovemaking has concluded."

He knew this from experience, not because he was a physician. My lover was no backward boy. "Sounds a bit messy."

He bent near to whisper in my ear. "Not as messy as childbirth."

What struck me about this conversation was its casual intimacy. Some of St. Sevier's ease with vocabulary was medical. As a physician, he had doubtless explained the use of the sponge to many men, and doubtless to a few women.

But our discussion wasn't clinical. It was just another bedtime conversation with a man I increasingly cherished for reasons that multiplied by the day—and night.

"Why would the Wood have a large store of these sponges?" I asked, rising to pass St. Sevier a dressing gown.

"Because it has a large staff. You heard young Mr. Green. He's enjoying a moonlit stroll with somebody, and he's not the only one."

"This is why there are no babies?" I asked. "Because everybody is using sponges?" There were babies, in the village apparently. A dame school educated children of many ages.

"Sponges are something every woman ought to have knowledge of. Babies coming one right after the other, when a family has limited means, is a recipe for misery and death."

I kissed St. Sevier's cheek and looped my arms around his waist. "You don't think the arrival of babies is God's will?"

"No god worth the name would will that innocent babies starve to death."

Hugh's voice was so bleak that I knew he spoke from experience in this too. "You truly must return to the practice of medicine, St. Sevier."

He held me, his cheek against my temple. I loved the fit of our bodies, loved the warmth of his embrace. His affection wasn't for show or to manipulate me into granting him favors. It was genuine to Hugh St. Sevier, and worth more than rubies.

"You are quite clear on this point, Violet, but then, clarity of argument is typical of you."

A delicate reference to my tirade on the terrace. I refused to be distracted. "On the battlefield and in camp, you learned more medicine than most men learn in a lifetime. That knowledge begs to be put to use in a more cheerful setting. The starving babies haunt you—they should haunt us all—but you can do more about them than most."

"And you would not mind being married to a physician who breaks the English rules of medical practice?"

I eased away and turned down the quilts. "The topic of marriage is complicated for me, but I can tell you this: I would rather be married to a man happily practicing his vocation than married to a man longing to contribute but frustrating his ambitions for the sake of his wife's social standing."

As I leaned over the bed to flip the covers down on the other side, St. Sevier stroked me lightly on the bum.

"You are a barrister now, speaking in hypotheticals. Be warned, Violet, that I am a determined man, and my eye remains on the prize."

He stroked my derriere, the scoundrel, and a little of my sense of failure about the whole visit to the Wood eased. I had come to know St. Sevier better here, had learned about his past and gained new reasons to respect him.

That was time well spent.

And yet, I thought of Carruthers, nearly consigned to risk his life in a fetid jail, waiting weeks for the assizes at which he might well have been sentenced to transportation—because Rutland thought it was time to make an example, *or to intimidate me into giving up.*

"Your mill wheel is turning at a great rate," St. Sevier said as we cuddled beneath the warmed blankets. "You are holding a mental court-martial and finding Rutland guilty of stupidity."

"Arrogance," I said, "but that man is not stupid. He proved his craftiness today. He's protecting the womenfolk at the Wood. That's the other side of his amorous coin. He genuinely cares for those under his protection, and he'd rather sack one or two at a time, on generous terms, than see his entire female staff..."

I fell silent as some wisp of a thought tried to coalesce in my brain. Something about Rutland's protectiveness, his frolics, his need to banish me before I jabbed my parasol into one hornet's nest too many... Why would he sacrifice even the Wood itself?

To protect the ladies, of course. He would do anything to keep the womenfolk at the Wood safe. But the ladies were not in any jeopardy, were they?

St. Sevier's thumb brushed the underside of my breast, and my mind tossed aside its conjectures. "St. Sevier?"

"I beg your pardon. You are still indisposed, and I ought not to impose on you."

"I am not indisposed," I said, shifting over him, "and it is not an imposition." Not from him, not ever from him.

CHAPTER THIRTEEN

"They don't want to see you go," Lucy said, folding a shawl over my traveling valise.

My trunks had been sent down at first light, and I had only the ordeal of breakfast to endure before leaving the Wood. I hated to think a puzzle had eluded my attempts to find a solution, but then, the owner of the Wood himself was determined to thwart me.

"Who doesn't want to see me go?" I asked, examining my reflection in the cheval mirror.

"The staff. The lot from the stable told the others what happened on the terrace, with Mr. Carruthers. The talk is... of leaving. All of them, though they call it 'mustering out.'"

I wore a carriage dress of dark blue wool. Perhaps too hot for the stuffy confines of the coach, perhaps not warm enough if the weather turned bleak.

"The whole staff would leave?" I asked.

"They can't all leave, but the hotels and hostels are hiring, and much of the inside staff could find work at least through summer."

"So they aren't undertaking an investigation of the problems on their own?" Though when would they have time? The Wood was understaffed for its size and overstaffed for its purse.

"They have tried to investigate, in their way," Lucy said. "They set a watch in the stable because they don't know who is causing the trouble. The footmen and maids took to working in pairs three months ago because that protects everybody from suspicion. Even the night porter prefers that a footman be on duty with him, because they are all so worried about false accusations."

The usual reason for staff to work in pairs was to reduce the incidence of theft and also to keep the women safer from the men who employed them. Those reasons hadn't been compelling at the Wood.

"The entire staff has no clue about who might be responsible?" They'd said as much when talking to me, of course, but Lucy would overhear much more honest gossip than I could hope to.

"Upjohn says the same thing. The lot of them are frustrated and anxious, even when it's just the footmen dicing in the hall. They don't know who is causing all the trouble, but they know it's not them."

Whom did that leave? The question had nearly come tripping out of my mouth when another query stepped before it.

"Lucy, did you ever find the third Mary White?"

She gathered up my brush, comb, and mirror from the vanity. "There's only the two. I asked the cook how many Mary Whites on her staff, then the housekeeper how many Mary Whites on her staff. They each said one."

"And you only ever found one Jenny Smith?"

Lucy paused in rearranging the contents of my valise, my mirror in her hand. "Jenny Smith is an undechambermaid, family wing. Stout, quiet, a hard worker, and fond of Jemmy Green in the stable."

Three ideas collided in my mind: The stringent economies forced on the staff at the Wood, the abundance of extramarital liaisons among the residents, and the lack of children. As I regarded my reflection in the mirror—a woman who appeared to stand quietly in a room that appeared to exist—an outlandish, entirely logical sequence of possibilities arranged itself in my mind.

The woman in the mirror wasn't real, and neither was the third Mary White.

"Please send a footman to fetch Mr. and Mrs. Jones for breakfast. If they ask, tell them it's a show of hospitality and civility toward Rutland's departing guests."

"Are you sure, my lady? We can be in the coaches and down the drive in less than an hour."

"I am already in disgrace, Lucy. I can't help that, but I refuse to leave here allowing Rutland to think he's outsmarted me."

That I would go toe to toe with a retired and titled colonel, under his own roof, when he'd all but cast me from the house, was surprising even to me. Rutland was in a desperate battle to maintain appearances at the Wood, and he was destined to lose unless I rode to his rescue.

I did not care half so much about Rutland, a grown man in great good health, as I did about the staff and the ladies who called the Wood home. For their sakes, I would not merely poke another hornet's nest before I left, I would smash it to bits.

St. Sevier met me on the stairs a half hour later. "Good morning. You are in a tempest."

"Good day." He cut a delicious figure in his riding attire, though I hardly had time to admire him. "Do you mean I am in a temper?"

"*Non.* You do occasionally grow annoyed, but you are ready to storm the breakfast parlor."

"I know who is causing the difficulties here at the Wood."

He offered his arm and escorted me down the steps at too decorous a pace. "Not Carruthers."

"Everybody knows Carruthers is innocent. That's why Rutland made an example of him."

Sebastian joined us at the foot of the steps. "Do I detect a one-woman firing squad in the person of your dear self, my lady?"

"I will aim the truth at Rutland, and if he is still determined to drum me out of the regiment, I will go peacefully and keep my mouth shut about what I've seen here."

St. Sevier paused as we crossed the cavernous foyer. "Might you share the truth with us first, Violet?"

I sketched for them what I'd worked out, though I knew the picture was far from complete. I was confident of my conclusions, though, and hoped the rest of the story would become apparent once I'd aired my theories before Rutland.

Neither man attempted to argue with me, which further bolstered my confidence.

"Rutland won't want to hear any of this," Sebastian said. "It does not reflect well on his household."

"Am I to hold my tongue for the sake of a man's vanity?" I retorted.

"His vanity, no," Sebastian said, "but do try to have a care for his pride, Violet. You and he are not so very different."

I had no idea what Sebastian meant by that remark, and we had reached the breakfast parlor. Garth and Daphne Jones were at the sideboard, Mr. Jones holding the plates while his lady wife filled them, as if they were at the buffet for a grand ball.

"Good morning, all," I said, nodding to the assemblage. Rutland and his lady occupied the head and foot of the table, respectively. The O'Deas sat along one side, the MacNeils the other. I served myself some eggs while subdued versions of morning greetings were exchanged all around. The only place remaining at the table was at Rutland's right hand, so there I did sit.

"You have a pretty day for your journey," Lady Rutland began, too brightly. "One hopes the weather will hold for you all the way to London."

The weather. The first and last resort of all persons who sought to advance the cause of civility—or mendacity. If I were a different sort of woman, the sort of woman Freddie Belmaine had married all those years ago, I might have returned a comment on the state of English roads, or the beauty of springtime.

"When I do reach London," I said, "I will have little to say about my visit at the Wood, other than to admire the scenery. Your secrets are safe with me, and I know I speak for St. Sevier and Lord Dunkeld in that regard. You may trust our discretion utterly."

Sebastian closed the parlor door and resumed his seat at Lady Rutland's right hand.

"We have no secrets," Rutland retorted, though he tried for a mild tone. "Planting will soon be upon us, and entertaining visitors at this time of year puts a strain on the staff."

"You hardly plant enough acres to keep your horses in oats," I countered. "But that is not relevant to the instant discussion. There are only two Mary Whites."

Lord Rutland looked at me as if I'd switched abruptly into Mandarin. "I beg your pardon?"

"The wage list for the female inside staff lists three Mary Whites. There are only two. There is only one Jenny Smith. I suspect if you looked over the pensioners' list, you'd find one or two fictitious names among the widows too. Maybe the laundresses include an apprentice who doesn't exist. Call them ghosts. I suspect they joined the payroll about the same time as all the frolicking began."

Rutland's gaze became positively arctic. "A lady does not refer in conversation to certain topics."

"A gentleman does not propose that his inability to sire children be solved by lending his wife out to his friends, not unless that gentleman is desperate and the lady willing."

Somebody—Milly MacNeil, Lady Rutland?—made a noise closely resembling a moan.

Rutland rose. "Dunkeld, St. Sevier, escort this woman from my home. Now."

Both of my menfolk remained seated, to their credit, while Daphne Jones reached for her husband's hand.

"The smallpox would be my guess," St. Sevier said quietly. "It can render a man sterile, as can chicken pox, measles, mumps, or the various venereal curses. So many soldiers were willing to surrender their lives for Britain. The army thanked them by establishing camps full of diseases that stole the ability to procreate from many of those not killed outright in battle. A high price to pay for patriotism."

Nobody looked at anybody, so I took up the charge.

"The Wood lacks an heir of the body, just as the MacNeils, Joneses, and O'Deas lack children. Lord Rutland took note of that situation and proposed an attempted remedy: switch partners, and perhaps nature would smile on one or more of the ladies. Who is to say the gentlemen alone bear responsibility for the lack of progeny? Try a yeld mare with a different stud and she'll sometimes get in foal. This approach is not unheard of among the aristocracy, whose family wealth largely depends on legitimate male children showing up in each generation."

"You know nothing," Rutland said, sounding more weary than affronted. "You need not air the rest of your theories, and that's all they are. Outlandish, female fancies."

"The ladies were willing at first," I said, "and one surmises you gave them a choice. The affection among you all is deep and genuine. The goal was worthy, even if the means of attaining it are unconventional."

Rutland scrubbed his hand over his face. "Will somebody make her hush?"

Nobody could make me hush. Not now, perhaps never again. "I speak up because I suspect you have stopped listening to your womenfolk, my lord. At some point, the ladies gave up on your scheme, or it became distasteful to them."

Rutland peered at his wife, who met his gaze steadily. Something painful and sweet passed between them, understood only by them.

The quality of the silence shifted, from fraught, to patient to resigned.

"They never objected," Rutland said at length. "They never said one word of protest. The ladies understand. They wanted children too. Athena still wants children. What good is it to marry a landed man if he can't also produce children to inherit the property and comfort their mother in her old age?"

Milly MacNeil glowered at our host. "We told you we would try it for three months, Rutland. *Three months.* There were to be rules, names drawn, Wednesday nights only. But at the end of three months, your blessed rules were a memory, and the lot of you were carrying on like you hadn't had leave in three years."

"And we've had no babies," Kathleen O'Dea said. "Not a one, and not for lack of trying on your parts. I told Pat I'd had enough. I would rather be his wife than anybody's doxy, or I wouldn't have married him."

"Lass," Tommie MacNeil said, "you're nobody's doxy, but you try telling Rutland his great plan isn't working. How long do you think your darling Pat would remain employed here? How long do you think I'd be kept on as steward if I hinted that my employer had run daft and traded our marriages for a mess of pottage? We embarked on the plan with the assent of our wives, then we were riding a tiger, as it were. Four tigers."

Milly MacNeil looked as if she did not know whether to laugh or cuff her husband's ear. "You mounted up enthusiastically enough, Tommie, me lad."

He shrugged. "As did you."

"We didn't," Lady Rutland muttered. "Not after the first three months. We complied—we love our husbands, and we are loyal to them—and that's not the same thing as enthusiasm."

"Hence," I said, "you hired the third Mary White."

Rutland sent me the sort of look reserved for dung heaps on hot days. "What *are* you going on about?"

"I'm talking about women exercising what authority remained to them." I said. "The ladies were reluctantly willing for the agreed-upon three months. You presumed on their good natures thereafter, though I grant you their protestations might have been private and ambiguous."

"Kathleen wasn't ambiguous," Patrick O'Dea said. "She cut me off at New Year's, so to speak, and I could not blame her. We should have just gone home to Ireland, but I was too... I did not want to feel like a deserter when the Wood was having such difficulties."

Garth Jones still held Daphne's hand. "Tell us about this Mary White."

"I'll tell you," Lady Rutland said. "Milly handles all the pay packets for the female staff. We simply invented some extra female staff. Four originally, but then you, Tommie, decided to sack Tamsin Henley because she was the last hired, and his lordship was imposing more economies."

"I hate damned economies," Tommie muttered.

"We all do," Lady Rutland replied, "but Milly was clever enough to carry through everything—the allowances for beer, tea, and candles, the cost of a maid's outfit and boots—and putting extra women on the staff resulted in some coin flowing to us in addition to our pin money. We have two extra widows on the pensioners' rolls, and there's a fictitious assistant to the seamstress getting a packet too."

Rutland had aged ten years in five minutes. "You *stole* from the Wood?"

Lady Rutland shook her head. "You would not listen. I told you the plan had been worth a try, but it didn't bear fruit. Rather than blow retreat and call it a lark, you..."

"Linen closets," Daphne Jones said wearily. "The conservatory. The gazebo. We weren't left in peace anywhere, and while it's amusing in a peculiar sort of way, it's also pathetic and just plain *tiresome*."

"If I'm going to have tiresome relations," Millicent said, "I'd like to have them with my own husband, in our bed behind a locked door. Not very adventurous of me, but then, I had hoped I married a solid, steady, unadventurous sort of man."

"You did, lass," Tommie said, his smile sad. "You did."

"I married a good man," Daphne Jones said. "I am still married to a good man, and while the rest of you fellows are dear and dashing and all that, I will simply deal with a lack of children rather than engage in any more pointless debauches."

"Which brings us," I said, "to the tallow candles at the holiday open house."

"Please do explain," Rutland said. "I assumed MacNeil had suggested tallow as an economy, but the stench was embarrassing."

Lady Rutland poured herself a cup of tea, an incongruously normal activity in the middle of one of the most peculiar conversations I'd ever participated in.

"The first sackings happened in November," Lady Rutland said. "I had considered using some tallow candles—lighting the ballroom is quite costly—but then Kathleen suggested that if the footmen were perceived to have disobeyed orders or fumbled badly, they might be next in line to lose their posts."

"We have too many," Millicent said. "Footmen, that is. Every private who could stay sober long enough to find his way here was put in livery if he asked prettily."

I expected Rutland to remonstrate with her over that conclusion, but he remained quiet.

"We dented the piano for good measure," Kathleen said. "Another bad reflection on the footmen, but nobody appeared to notice."

Garth Jones accepted the teapot from Lady Rutland. "Thus you slashed the brigadier and whatnot?"

"I hate that portrait," Lady Rutland said. "It doesn't even look like Grandpapa."

"Consign it to the attics," I said, "but that doesn't explain how an entire batch of cream was ruined."

"Tommie?" Kathleen held out a plate of jam tarts to him. "Any ideas about that?"

He took the plate, but did not serve himself. "You saw me?"

"I saw you going into the dairy," she said. "If you are sneaking into the dairy at midafternoon, *alone*, you aren't up to any good."

MacNeil offered the tarts to his wife, who also declined.

"The officers sought to defend the enlisted men," I said. "Mac-Neil ruined the cream to throw suspicion back on the female staff. Hence the problems escalated, with the officers trying to cast the maids into the shade, and the ladies making war on the enlisted men. I suspect the ladies dis-arranged the saddle room and turned the sheep loose in the garden, while the gents broke figurines and scorched curtains. Was the coach wheel an accident?"

"Of course it was. We would never—" Lady Rutland began, but her husband speared her with a look.

"You turned the bedamned sheep loose in the garden. Why, Athena? I paid a fortune for those rubbishing tulips because you said you loved the colors."

She set her teacup down very carefully. "You listen to me when I say I love the bright colors of the Holland bulbs, but you ignore me when I tell you I've had enough of conducting myself like a camp follower. Had you asked me, I would have told you that a few window boxes would have been a lovely gesture.

"I love you, Damien," she went on, "but *you do not listen.* Your stubbornness about larking from bed to bed made us determined to keep a bit of coin back. I have enough saved that we ladies can take a *prolonged* repairing lease in Edinburgh if you continue to insist on a frolic that has outlived its usefulness."

We were back to nobody looking at anybody, though I hoped for the sake of all involved that Lady Rutland's husband was at least listening to her.

"Why haven't you already left?" I asked.

Millicent addressed her comment to Tommie. "We did not feel we could honorably quit the field. Half the maids would be sacked in our absence or another carpet of tulips laid down."

"We don't really want to go," Kathleen O'Dea added quietly.

"We want our marriages to be ours again, and for our husbands to listen to us."

"It's not about the money," Daphne added. "We've all managed on short rations and made do in tents, for pity's sake. We simply didn't see any other way to make our point."

"How much have you ladies saved?" I asked.

Lady Rutland named a figure that would not solve the Wood's problems, but suggested strongly that over time—with common sense and cooperation—those problems could be solved.

"We will turn it over to you gladly," Lady Rutland informed her husband, "but you must listen to us, my lord. The war is over, and we are wives, not subalterns and recruits. It's your money. Besides, if we feel a need to abandon the Wood in future, we will impose on Lady Violet's hospitality."

"You ladies will be most welcome," I said. "*Most* welcome, but I suspect you truly do want to see that money put to use here at the Wood."

All four ladies spoke as one. "We do."

"That is…" Rutland stared hard at his empty plate. "That is impressive. I quibble with the means, but can commend the motive and the initiative. If the ladies will excuse us, I'd like a word with the gentlemen in the library. St. Sevier, Dunkeld, you will join us."

The officers made a dignified retreat, leaving an odd, relieved silence behind.

Daphne Jones held up the pretty porcelain teapot. "More tea, anybody?"

CHAPTER FOURTEEN

"You will think us all quite wanton," Lady Rutland observed when the women had gathered at her end of the table. "We thought we were, too, at first."

"We were noble and naughty at the same time," Kathleen said, "lending out our husbands to one another, while enduring attentions we never had to admit we enjoyed."

"Our husbands are a considerate bunch." Daphne had brought the jam tarts with her to the foot of the table and offered me first pick. "The fellows made the business easy to endure."

"Pleasurable," Daphne said. "We must allow that much. They were eager and bashful and exerted themselves to be winsome."

I ought to have been overcome with mortification to hear such confessions, but I was also, truly... fascinated.

"Wasn't it awkward?" I asked.

"A bit, at first," Millicent said, "but we are friends before all else. I helped nurse Rutland when he had smallpox because I had the disease as a child. I'd seen him many times as God made him, heard him curse fate, and seen him too weak to even curse. I wasn't going to let him die, and he wasn't going to abandon his post. That creates a bond."

"Tommie ended up in the infirmary," Daphne said. "Out of his head with fever from a French ball through the arm. He thought I was Milly for a while, told me all manner of things. Garth has admired Athena for years, and yet, he never once strayed until Rutland came up with this scheme. I did not begrudge my husband a few harmless interludes with somebody who would never try to tempt him away from me."

"Garth is romantic and tender and never in a hurry," Lady Rutland said. "Fine qualities in a man, but he's not my Damien."

"Patrick," Daphne said, "can make me laugh. He's lighthearted and affectionate about everything, and I do mean everything. I treasure that about him, but I want my Garth back."

"Tommie," Kathleen said, "is inventive. The places that man has accosted me and the things he knows... You did marry an adventurous man, Milly, adventurous in the nicest possible way, but I have had enough adventures in the springhouse, the dairy, the saddle room, and the gazebo."

I ought to have stuffed a jam tart in my mouth, or three jam tarts, rather than give way to vulgar curiosity. "What of Rutland?"

Millicent looked around the table. "Stamina," she said solemnly. "His lordship has been generously endowed with stamina."

This provoked a round of merriment and a smug smile from Lady Rutland. "What of St. Sevier, Lady Violet? Surely you have sampled his charms?"

Oh dear. The ladies were regarding me with such frank, good-hearted curiosity, I had to give them some sort of answer.

"I am a proper, boring widow, and I would not for one moment admit to having strayed from strictest decorum with my escort," I said, which provoked some hooting and laughter. "But if I did, I would expect St. Sevier to be romantic, unhurried, lighthearted on some occasions, inventive on others, possessed of prodigious stamina, and blessed with an endless capacity for tenderness." All wonderfully true, and my smile very likely confirmed it.

"We suspected as much," Lady Rutland said. "He was never *available*, if you take my meaning, but he looks like he wants to be available to you."

"So does Dunkeld," Daphne said. "I knew I could accost them both without fear that my overtures would be reciprocated."

Milly bit into a tart. "Trying to make Garth jealous?"

"Jealous, angry, determined... anything but complacent. Garth acceded to Rutland's plan because he thought I wanted a baby that badly, but upon considerable reflection, I would rather not have a child whose paternity is open to question. Garth could apparently live with raising a child if the father was Patrick, Tommie, or Rutland, but what of Dunkeld's child? St. Sevier's? But Garth just grew quieter, and he's devilish quiet to begin with."

The tarts were rapidly disappearing, and I felt as if we were just getting to the heart of the matter.

"If you return to your respective marital beds, that solves one set of difficulties," I said, and for me, those were the most important concerns, "but the Wood is still in a precarious financial state."

"The problem," said Millicent, "is the price of wool."

"The problem," Daphne countered darkly, "is the price of supporting a private army. Most of the staff are hard workers, and heaven knows they've put up with short rations, but they look to the Wood as they looked to the military—as a provider of everything for the rest of their lives."

"We want to do that," Lady Rutland said, swiping her finger through a streak of jam on her plate, "but we haven't the coin. Rutland is so concerned for our finances that he nearly told St. Sevier not to come calling with Lady Violet. The kitchen has exerted itself because we have company—at long last, company!—and we've raided the cellars for the last of the decent vintages, and still, our hospitality has been barely adequate."

"What would you do if you had the coin?" I asked, the question half idle, though somebody needed to think beyond tallow candles and pinched pennies.

"Such menus," Lady Rutland said, sitting up. "The army teaches you how to cook for a throng without spending a fortune, else we would have long since starved. It doesn't take much to make mutton and potatoes into a company meal. Applesauce, a few bites of capon, a fish soup—we have fish aplenty here—dress it up with relishes and sauces and finish with a rich dessert. The guests are full, they recall the dessert fondly, and they don't notice the nightcap was a mediocre vintage."

"What of the grounds?" I asked. "They require tremendous effort to maintain, do they not?"

"The sheep graze the park," Kathleen O'Dea said. "The walking paths are ancient and need little maintenance. The back gardens and the conservatory are an effort, and the kitchen garden requires a lot of work, but Patrick made sure the greater grounds mostly look after themselves. Groundsmen cost money."

Everything cost money, and yet, the Wood was lovely. The gazebo, the bluebell wood, the little parlor set up in the conservatory, the back gardens...

"I have an idea," I said, "but you must not allow the men to think this idea came from me. Rutland will have the notion shot at dawn if he thinks I had a hand in it."

"If this idea turns the Wood into a viable estate," Lady Rutland said, "he will do no such thing. Tell us, Lady Violet, and be quick about it."

I spoke at length, embellishing extempore on what was little more than the seed of a plan. The ladies caught my enthusiasm, and by the time the gentlemen rejoined us, we were chattering madly, talking over one another, and ringing for more tarts and tea.

～

"I am sorry to see you go," Lord Rutland said, bowing over my hand as the coach horses stomped in the traces. "I was also sorry to see you arrive, so perhaps my penance is just."

When he smiled, his charm came through, and he owned a quantity of charm. "I might make a return visit," I said, "as a paying guest."

He bent near. "Be merciful, my lady. Give us a year or two to get the place running up to standards, and by then, we will be worthy of your custom. I know nothing of the hotelier's craft, but my wife has faith in my ability to manage the endeavor, and my staff has taken to her idea with enthusiasm."

"You are richly blessed in your spouse, my lord."

"And in my staff. You'd think we were planning another campaign, over the mountains and into France. What of you, my lady? What lies ahead for you and our good doctor?"

St. Sevier was at the mounting block, conferring with Sebastian about I knew not what. I would winkle that information from St. Sevier in the first five miles of our southward journey. Lady Rutland stood on the terrace with the rest of the send-off committee. We had made our farewells with promises to remain in touch by letter, and that was a promise I would keep.

"We continue on to London and will reunite with Lord Dunkeld on the occasion of my nephew's christening a few weeks hence." I was already looking forward to that gathering, and not simply as an excuse to leave London again. "Dunkeld and I are to be godparents."

Rutland linked arms with me, resting his fingers over my hand at his elbow. "The poor man was mad for you when I first met him. Sick with frustration because he hadn't been allowed to offer for you. Damned near got himself killed, but as the army often does, we promoted him for bravery when we ought to have reprimanded him for foolishness."

"You refer to Lord Dunkeld?"

"Of course I do. If you knew how many letters he wrote to you and tossed in the fire... Part of my initial antipathy toward you was because, last I'd heard, you were unwilling to entertain the suit of a man so clearly smitten and so obviously worthy, and you married a wealthy, fribbling cit instead. I have my lowly title, your ladyship, but I believe in merit as well as birthright, and MacHeath, as we knew him then, was and is a fine man."

A footman set my valise inside the traveling coach, the slower, heavier baggage coach having already departed.

"What was the rest of your initial antipathy toward me?"

"May I be frank?" Rutland said.

"Please. I fear we are to be friends, Rutland, and I demand honesty from my familiars."

He drew my shawl up around my shoulders. "I adore fierce women and am particularly drawn to fierce women with abundant curves and lovely, intelligent eyes. You looked at me, and all I could think was, 'St. Sevier is a damned lucky man if he can hold on to her, but he'll have his hands full.'"

"Did it occur to you that I would have my hands full with St. Sevier?"

"Fierce," Rutland said again. "You would have done well as an officer's wife."

I patted his hand. "I would have done better as an officer. Occupy yourself with holding on to Lady Rutland, sir, for I will expect a full report from her when I return next year."

By mutual consent, I gathered, the noble, ridiculous, naughty infidelity had been brought to a halt—romping by fiat wasn't as much fun as anticipated—and all hands were now turned to making the Wood the premier destination for hillwalkers of means and discernment.

Before Rutland could offer me a rejoinder, St. Sevier stalked away from the mounting block, swearing in French about why wasn't his horse already secured to the boot and—*mon Dieu!*—why must he see to everything himself, without exception, on every occasion.

St. Sevier was clearly upset to be leaving his old friends.

"The northern air agrees with your Frenchman," Sebastian said, running his stirrup down the leather. "You will take good care of him, methinks."

"He takes good care of me."

Sebastian patted his horse, a great dark beast whom he'd ridden to war. "I know. I will cheerfully kill him if his attentiveness ever lapses."

"You've told St. Sevier that?"

"He knows," Sebastian said darkly. "I detest farewells, so please be about your scolds, and I will see you in a few weeks when we dunk your brother's wee bairnie."

"I haven't any scolds." Nor could I read Sebastian's mood. "I am endlessly grateful to you for coming when I needed you, and I will worry about you and miss you until next we meet."

He ceased petting his horse and offered me a crooked smile. "You know how to wound a man, Violet Belmaine. I will miss you, too, but next time you have need of me, please send for me yourself. I would rather heed your summons than St. Sevier's."

"I did not grasp the military protocol, while he did, and I would not have wanted to bother you."

Sebastian caught me up in a tight hug. "Bother me, Violet. If you ever have need of me, bother me. Please. I want your promise."

I could barely breathe for the snugness of his embrace. "I promise. I will send for you myself."

He let me go with a kiss to my cheek. "Best news I've heard all day. Ask St. Sevier about investing in the hotel."

"You will be careful?" I asked as Sebastian swung into the saddle. "Don't eat the typical inn fare if it tastes at all questionable. Pack comestibles in the morning, but no meat. The weather is growing too warm for that. Don't forget to water your horse often, and if it rains, halt your journey for a day or two. Your bride hunting has waited this long, it can wait another few days rather than put you at risk for an ague."

Sebastian leaned down and kissed me on the mouth. "God, I will miss you." He kneed his horse away from the mounting block, waved to the crowd on the terrace, and cantered away down the drive.

I hated to see him go. Hated it, but consoled myself that at least this time, he wasn't off to fight a war, merely to find a bride, which errand I could not possibly object to.

At all.

"You will see the marquess again soon," St. Sevier said as his gelding was tied to the back of the coach. "Now please let us be off before my legendary good nature is tried past all bearing by another round of good wishes and sly innuendos."

"Sly innuendos?"

He led me over to the coach, pausing as the footman let down the steps. "I do not know what you told those women, but my handsome derrière has never received so many fond pats as I have endured in the past fifteen minutes. I have never been winked at so excessively, and in my entire life—"

"You have never enjoyed being a guest of the regiment as thoroughly. We are welcome back at any time, St. Sevier. You and your derrière are held in great affection here at the Wood, but please recall that I am not inclined to share treasures entrusted into my exclusive keeping."

The moment turned oddly serious, despite the farewells and *au revoirs* called from the terrace.

"Please get into the coach," St. Sevier said, "and do not make free with my person before the gawking mob." He offered our hosts a final wave good-bye and climbed in after me. "My heart is entrusted into your exclusive keeping, Violet. Do I gather you are allowing that arrangement to become reciprocal?"

When a woman lost her heart to a handsome, charming, honorable, passionate, absolutely lovely Frenchman, was that a matter of *allowing*?

"You state the obvious," I said as the coach lurched forward. "You are, as noted previously, irresistible."

"No, I am not. You have resisted me for months. Do not toy with me now, Violet. I have asked permission to court you because I cannot imagine my future without you in it. Where do I stand with you?"

He sat beside me, his gaze on the pastures beyond the window. We did not touch, but I could feel the pride in him and the stoicism. I would never know how much suffering he had seen or endured, but I didn't need to.

I knew he would brew me a tisane for my female complaints, hold me while I dreamed, defend me from every harm, and accompany me on every adventure. I knew I loved him, that he loved me, and that he was worthy of my love.

"I am not ready for marriage," I said, "not even ready for an engagement."

Hugh did not so much as glance at me. "Therefore?"

My heart began beating like a kettledrum, and my arms and nape felt the cool prickling that presaged an attack of nerves.

"Therefore, I had best develop an understanding with you, because if you allow another woman to do anything more than pat your handsome backside, I will have to call her out."

"An... understanding."

"An exclusive, intimate prelude to further commitments when the time is right."

He took off his hat and put it on the opposite bench, then undid my bonnet ribbons and set my millinery aside as well.

"What does this mean, Violet, an *understanding*?"

"I don't know if there's a comparable French term, but it means... you and I belong to each other. We will probably get married, barring the unforeseen, but my courage does not yet extend that far."

He laid an arm across my shoulders. "Your courage has grown somewhat in recent months?"

"Enormously, mostly thanks to you."

The coach turned left at the foot of the drive, and the horses picked up a faster trot. "You do not tell me what I want to hear, Violet."

"I tell you the truth. I am not ready for marriage, and I never want to lose you."

"And what of children?"

"If and when I marry, I will hope for children, but we both know I cannot promise... I have not carried successfully despite years of trying."

"Here we have an irony," he said. "The couples at the Wood were willing to relax their vows in hopes of conceiving. I am willing to speak vows with you, despite the strong possibility that I, too, may never become a father. In the military, I contracted both measles and mumps, a common hazard of treating an ailing population. You deserve to know this, if we are to have an *understanding*."

I cuddled closer, wanting to spare him the heartache of his admission. He loved children, he was unlikely to have any of his own, and yet, he was prepared to marry me, and I was a poor bet as a broodmare.

"We have an understanding, St. Sevier. From this moment forward, we have an understanding."

He held me loosely, and we talked for the next several miles about the terms upon which he and Sebastian had invested in Lord and Lady Rutland's hotel venture at the Wood. They would cater to veterans and military families on leave, of course, and offer all the little flourishes and comforts particularly prized by such guests.

I gradually dozed off in St. Sevier's arms, certain in my heart that our frolic in the Lakes had been a worthwhile adventure indeed.

I was still not looking forward to my return to London, but I was cheered by the prospect of the christening a few weeks hence. Little did I know that my adventures were far from over and that considerably more courage would soon be required of me.

But that, as they say, is a tale for another time.

TO MY DEAR READERS

If you haven't traveled to the Lake District, please consider adding that to your bucket list, if only virtually. Beatrix Potter of bunny rabbit fame did much to conserve the traditional farming way of life in the Lakes, and was herself an award-winning sheep breeder. Upon her death, she left fourteen farms and more than 4000 acres to the National Trust the better to preserve what she most valued about this beautiful part of the world.

The alpine forests we see there today are largely modern replantings, but they were created to reproduce the ecosystem native to the area before deforestation became such a scourge.

I will never forget traveling west from Yorkshire to catch my first glimpse of the Lakes. Crossing Yorkshire, I thought, "Well, the scenery is lovely. Sheep, hills, hills, sheep, and oh, look, stone walls!" To me, that is truly delightful countryside. Then the landscape abruptly changed, going a little bit Highland, a little bit fairy tale, and I was enthralled.

But, like Lady Violet, Sebastian, and St. Sevier, I could not tarry in the north indefinitely. Lady Violet's next adventure sees her back at the Deerfield family seat—not her fave place in the whole world—

but at least she's accompanied by her two fave fellows. I've included an excerpt from **Lady Violet Holds a Baby** below.

I'm releasing the first six Lady Violet mysteries at once, though I suspect there will be more tales in this series. Going forward, I won't stockpile a half dozen titles before publishing. And of course, I'm also still writing romances—waves to Ned and Rosalind from ***Never a Duke***, which comes out in April. Though it is coincidence that my next **Rogues to Riches** title also has a bit of a mystery plot?

If you'd like to stay up to date on all my releases, discounts, and pre-orders, following me on **Bookbub** is probably the easiest way to do that. I also have a **Deals** page on my website, which I update about monthly, and that lists any sales, early releases, or freebie, especially those happening on the **web store**. If you're inclined toward **newsletters**, I publish one about every month or so, and I promise that unsubscribing is easy. Also, I will never sell, spam, or swap your addie.

However you prefer to keep in touch, I wish you always...

Happy reading!

Grace Burrowes

Read on for an excerpt from **Lady Violet Holds a Baby**!

LADY VIOLET HOLDS A BABY— EXCERPT

Chapter One

A handsome, passionate, *inventive* Frenchman was subtly inviting me to sample his charms.

"Perhaps later, St. Sevier."

My traveling companion affected gentlemanly puzzlement. "You give me the look a farm wife aims at the father of her eleven children when I merely suggest we fold out the benches for greater comfort. What is amiss with my darling Violet?"

"I don't feel very darling." The traveling coach rocked along while I pondered my own understatement. My late husband would have called my mood shrewish, but then, *shrewish* was one of many pejoratives for which no exact male counterpart had been invented —yet.

In my present mood, I felt up to the challenge of remedying that oversight.

"You face the prospect of another family gathering," St. Sevier said, settling an arm around my shoulders. "This challenge would daunt Napoleon's bravest cuirassiers. I myself would not venture into the company of the Deerfields without your stalwart escort."

My Deerfield family consisted of my four older brothers, two of whom were married, and my father, the Earl of Derwent. I could also claim some aunties and cousins, as well as a pair of nieces and one infant nephew.

That I knew of. Given my father's propensity for rascally behavior, I might have legions of half-siblings about whom I was ignorant. At least one of my brothers had sired a by-blow, as had my late husband. Papa dismissed his roguish deportment as reminiscent of an earlier era, and I had no reason to believe he'd changed with the times.

Why my thoughts should wander to my father's flirtations I did not know.

"Shall I read to you?" St. Sevier asked. "You can explain Byron to me. He does not translate easily to the French."

"No Byron, thank you." His lordship's verse was exquisitely witty, also savagely bitter. Having not yet reached my thirtieth year, and enjoying great good health as well as the devoted company of a dear man, I was not entitled to bitterness.

Nonetheless, my mood had that acrid, seething quality often associated with bitterness. My appetite had grown indifferent in recent days, and I had neither the energy for much activity nor the ability to sleep well.

"St. Sevier, how does one know if a bout of melancholia is descending?"

Hugh's embrace became subtly protective. He was a skilled physician who'd also done service as a battlefield surgeon with Wellington's troops—despite having French antecedents. I had come to know St. Sevier as more than a passing acquaintance when the time had come for me to emerge from mourning.

I'd found myself barely able to emerge from my own house.

For two years, that dwelling had been more a prison than a refuge. Nonetheless, when I'd finally completed my second year of mourning, I became inexplicably fearful of venturing out even to attend divine services.

Hugh, whose path had crossed mine on one of my rare social outings, had suggested I start by reading at a window, if that was all I could manage. From there, I graduated to taking tea with him on the terrace, and then we'd strolled the garden while we discussed the many books I'd read in the previous two years.

I had known St. Sevier prior to my bereavement as a passing acquaintance, but in widowhood, his strolls with me in the garden had become an escort to church or a carriage ride in the park. Then the blighter had coaxed me into attending some of the less glittering social occasions to which an earl's widowed daughter was invariably invited.

Hugh St. Sevier was tenacious, wily, relentless, and kind. In the year since I'd resumed a life beyond mourning, he and I had shared several adventures and grown close enough that he had asked me to become his wife.

I was tempted. Hugh was everything estimable in a man, as my late husband had not been. Hugh was also affectionate, and I needed that almost more than I'd needed those walks in the garden. My late spouse, Freddie Belmaine, had been cut from the same self-indulgent cloth as my father, for all that Freddie had been an outwardly attentive spouse. He'd offered me his arm when he escorted me. He'd parted from me with a peck on my cheek and shown me reasonable consideration in bed.

I did not miss Freddie, but neither did I hate him. He'd done the best he could, as had I, and no more need be said on the matter.

"One does not always know when a bout of melancholia is descending," St. Sevier said. "Melancholia is unlike a sick headache, where narrowed vision, distorted hearing, or a sensitivity to light can presage the onset of pain. Melancholia is diabolical. It can announce its approach with excessive good spirits, with fatigue, with unexplained tears, with no signs at all. Could you not simply be in the grip of a slight case of dread, Violet?"

Of all the many qualities I loved about Hugh—his humor, his compassion, his integrity—his willingness to simply talk to me was near the top of the list. Then too, he was a fine-looking man at slightly over six feet, with chestnut hair and brown eyes that could shine with humor, ire, or understanding.

"I don't dread my family." Did I dread this gathering? Did I wish the coachman would slow the team from a brisk trot to a walk?

"You regard your family with wary affection. I came to feel something similar for my late wife. I cared for her, I wanted her to be happy, but I suspected that sometimes her happiness and mine had an inverse relationship."

For a man whose native tongue was French, St. Sevier could wield English with impressive delicacy. "She enjoyed making you miserable?"

"We were young, and a jealous husband is a husband showing some regard for his wife. Ann and I married as a result of wartime expedience, and I had hoped we would grow to be friends. I was not the jealous sort, though—I was too tired to be jealous—and this vexed her exceedingly."

St. Sevier did not often speak of his past, which was understandable. As a French émigré who had volunteered to provide medical services to Wellington's army, that past was full of sorrows, conflicting loyalties, and regrets.

His three brothers had served under Napoleon, and not a one of them had survived the war.

"Did you dread your wife's company?" I asked, rather than return to the dreary topic of melancholia.

"I would go through my day in the infirmary and surgery, longing to return to the tent or billet I shared with her. I would grow famished for the domesticity of a meal taken with my wife rather than with the officers. I wove fancies about trading gossip, because men and the women in a military camp gossip differently, and yet, as the sun set, and the time came to rejoin her... I would dither."

"Because," I said, "you and she argued when you should have chatted. The meals were taken in silence, and nothing you did was ever good enough for your spouse. I was relieved when Freddie died."

After five years of marriage, we'd reached a truce that had grown colder with each passing season. Freddie had his numerous frolics, and I had my anger at him for enjoying the pleasures any man of means expected to indulge in. Seventeen-year-old brides were ripe for disillusionment.

Spoiled husbands brought that out in them.

"Ann hated army life," Hugh said, his gaze going to the lovely English countryside beyond the coach window. "Then she was widowed, then she married me rather than become a regimental commodity. I was not relieved when she abandoned me to make her way back to Scotland alone, but neither was I surprised."

"And when she did not make it home?" She'd been killed in an ambush, though details were vague. A French patrol? Spanish *guerrilleros*? Deserters? Brigands? Spain had been a cauldron of violence and shifting alliances for the duration of Wellington's campaign.

St. Sevier left off pretending to study fields, pastures, and endless stone walls. "I was sad to learn of Ann's death, Violet, but to make war is to make sadness, and the sadness in its way can be more deadly than the bullets. Let us turn our conversation to happier topics. Will Lord Dunkeld be on hand when we arrive at Derwent Hall?"

Sebastian MacHeath, Marquess of Dunkeld, was to be godfather to my new nephew. Sebastian had fought in Spain with my youngest brother, Felix, and spent many summers and school holidays racketing around rural Surrey with my siblings.

And with me. War was a less cheery topic than the present incarnation of Sebastian MacHeath, but only just. As a youth, he'd been my dearest friend—my only friend—and his decision to join up had vexed me sorely.

That decision had also vexed his titled uncle, the previous Marquess of Dunkeld, and at the time, I'd thought twitting the old marquess had been Sebastian's sole motivation.

"Lord Dunkeld was making the rounds in London," I said, "hunting a marchioness, no doubt. I've told him he ought to find himself a stalwart Scottish lass to fulfill that office, but he says they know better than to marry a man with a castle."

"Impossible to heat, expensive to maintain." Hugh kissed my temple, the exact sort of casual gesture I usually found so endearing from him. "Tell me of the rest of the gathering. Extended family? Neighbors, in-laws? I want the whole list, and please tell me your lady cousins have declined to attend."

My lady cousins had made St. Sevier's acquaintance on the occasion of Felix's wedding. To say they'd been smitten was an understatement. More accurate to label their reaction to Hugh as stricken with a dire case of hen-witted infatuation.

I had not been infatuated with Hugh, but I had been attracted to him. He had been wise enough to allow that interest to ripen into a deeper regard, one kiss, one embrace, one passionate night at a time.

"I'm not sure who all is expected," I said, "but as godmother, my presence is required. The house will doubtless be mobbed, because this is the earldom's next heir whose arrival we're celebrating."

I was overjoyed for Felix and Katie, who were besotted and not at all high in the instep. They would be loving parents to the boy and prevent my father from meddling overmuch in his grandson's upbringing.

"Is that what has you in such a brown study, Violet? Does the child cause you heartache?" Hugh asked, brushing his fingers along my cheek.

I closed my eyes, enjoying his caress. "Hmm?"

"Never mind," he said. Even with my eyes closed, I could sense the shift in the light that occurred when Hugh drew the coach's shades down. "Have a nap, and by the time you waken, we will be tooling up your father's drive."

Hugh had, in his gentle, oblique way, pointed me in the direction of a painful insight. Freddie had had his light-skirts, his commerce, his clubs, and his wagers. He'd had a by-blow or two, while I had had a household to manage and a husband who'd occasionally visited my bed.

And yet, after five years of marriage and two disappointments, to use the hideously genteel term, my nursery had still been empty.

Always, achingly empty.

Order your copy of **Lady Violet Holds a Baby**!

73016285R00116